Torn Shapes of Desire
Internet Erotica

MARY ANNE MOHANRAJ

with photographs by Tracy Lee

INTANGIBLE ASSETS MANUFACTURING
PHILADELPHIA

Torn Shapes of Desire: Internet Erotica
an Intangible Assets Manufacturing book

ISBN 1-885876-03-3
Library of Congress Catalog Card Number: 96-78899

Back cover author photo by Felice Macera, Inks, Inc.
Front cover photo and interior photos Copyright © 1996 by Tracy Lee
Cover design by Michael J. Levin.
Stories and Poems Copyright © 1992-1996 Mary Anne Mohanraj
Some Poems in "Jinsong" Copyright © 1994 Cecil Williams
Some stories and poems first appeared in print elsewhere: "Internet Erot-
ica Writers Interview" in Puritan Magazine, "Attraction" in Original Sin,
"Cobalt Blue" and "Unabashed Paean" in MAKAR, "Confession" in Lilac
Dawn, "Hymn" and "Confession" in EIDOS Magazine.

Intangible Assets Manufacturing
828 Ormond Avenue, Drexel Hill, PA 19026-2604
fax +1 610 853 3733
info@iam.com   http://www.iam.com

Printed in the United States of America
10 9 8 7 6 5 4 3 2 1

To Kevin, Lisette and Alex,
for love, support and criticism,

And to all my readers,
whose enthusiasm gave me the courage to continue.

ACKNOWLEGMENTS

As this is my first book, I have an awful lot of people to thank, and I'm going to try really hard to get them all, though I'll undoubtedly forget some. So here goes...

My parents—they may not quite appreciate all of what I do, but they always had complete faith in my ability to do it...

B.J. Smith and Luci Fortunato-De Lisle, two of the best teachers a very bookish high school student with impossible dreams of being a writer could have...

Writers and readers from my first newsgroups (alt.callahans, rec.arts.poems, rec.arts.erotica (back when Tim Pierce moderated it) and alt.sex.stories); their support helped me to believe that maybe I could write just a bit better than the average net.writer.wannabe...

The online Writers' Workshop, for hundreds of readings and critiques and encouragement (especially the then-moderator, Rheal Nadeau, of inexhaustible patience and good sense)...

John McMullen and Brian T., my able assistants in the Erotica Writers' Workshop, great friends, and impressive authors in their own right...

Dale L. Larson, Cecilia Tan, Gary Bowen and Jeff Chudyk, editors extraordinaire...

And finally, I must thank Dean, Manny, Kira, Paul, Mort, Kevin, Kirsten, Adam, Karina, Joe, Alex, Clive, Marek, Jeff, Michael, Bethany, Kathryn, David and Sherman. This would have been a very different book without their contributions....

TABLE OF CONTENTS

6

The Internet treats censorship as damage and routes around it. —John Gilmore

So long as I am in the White House, there will be no relaxation of the national effort to control and eliminate smut from our national life. —Richard Nixon

Damn all expurgated books; the dirtiest book of all is the expurgated book. —Walt Whitman

I am mortified to be told that, in the United States of America, the sale of a book can become a subject of inquiry, and of criminal inquiry too. —Thomas Jefferson

If art is to nourish the roots of our culture, society must set the artist free to follow his vision wherever it takes him. —John Fitzgerald Kennedy

The pillars of truth and the pillars of freedom—they are the pillars of society. —Henrik Ibsen

Every compulsion is put upon writers to become safe, polite, obedient, and sterile. —Sinclair Lewis

Nudity is the most natural state. I was born nude and I hope to be buried nude. —Elle MacPherson

Take off all your clothes and walk down the street waving a machete and firing an Uzi, and terrified citizens will phone the police and report: "There`s a naked person outside!" —Mike Nichols

There are those who so dislike the nude that they find something indecent in the naked truth. —F. H. Bradley

What spirit is so empty and blind, that it cannot recognize the fact that the foot is more noble than the shoe, and skin more beautiful than the garment with which it is clothed? —Michaelangelo

In America, sex is an obsession, in other parts of the world, it is a fact. —Marlene Dietrich

It's red hot, mate. I hate to think of this sort of book getting in the wrong hands. As soon as I've finished this, I shall recommend they ban it. —Tony Hancock

Obscenity is whatever happens to shock some elderly and ignorant magistrate. —Bertrand Russell

Not when truth is dirty, but when it is shallow, does the enlightened man dislike to wade into its waters. —Friedrich Nietzsche

When they took the 4th Amendment, I was quiet because I didn't deal drugs. When they took the 6th Amendment, I was quiet because I am innocent. When they took the 2nd Amendment, I was quiet because I don't own a gun. Now they have taken the 1st Amendment, and I can only be quiet. —Rick Kelly and Lyle Myhr

"Exon me!", she cried, as I licked her hot wet Gorton. She writhed under my teasing tongue as her Gramm washed over her, her juices pouring out. I moved up to suck and nibble her Heflins, only to have her clutch my Byrd, and drive my aching Helms into her waiting Gorton. "Coats!", she said, "We're being quoted in a political text!" —Anonymous on the Net

EDITOR'S FORWARD

I never thought I'd be publishing "dirty stories." It's not that I'm a prude, I was just surprised to find myself in a situation where the issue came up at all. I'm a software engineer turned computer publisher, so how'd I end up editing and publishing a book with "erotica" in the title? And why am I so proud of it?

For ten years, I've lived a significant portion of my life in cyberspace. In addition to using the net during those years, electronically communicating with people around the world, I've worked on some of the software the net is made with, consulted for people expanding the net, and I'm the author of a book and several articles about networking and the Internet. So I paid special attention when a few members of the far-right started pushing an awful net bill through the United States Congress. The so-called "Communications Decency Act" (CDA) attempts to reduce all material on the Internet to a level appropriate for children, making it impossible for adults to communicate about important issues.

A new law isn't needed. The net is already subject to the same laws against obscenity and child pornography that apply to any media. The Internet is interactive; you must set out to find what you're looking for. So adults can decide for themselves what they want to see. Parents can control what their children access on the net, by direct supervision or by software which denies access based on parental criteria. (Surfwatch and NetNanny, for example, not only have a set of categories they automatically screen for, but can also be tailored to avoid anything else a parent finds objectionable.)

The CDA criminalizes network speech that is constitutionally protected in print and available from any bookstore or library: material that is "indecent" or "patently offensive." Both terms are unconstitutionally vague (they have no absolute legal definition, referring to "community standards", what standards apply to a global Internet is not clear) and overbroad (less restrictive means would obtain the desired effect). The ridiculous result is that, for example, you could be jailed or fined for creating Web sites containing the full text of the Supreme Court's Pacifica Decision (which includes a transcript of George Carlin's "7 dirty words" that broadcasters aren't supposed to use). Not knowing exactly what might be indecent has an incredibly chilling effect, worse than the actual censorship itself. Law-abiding citizens are forced to second-guess the prosecutors, and must err on the side of the conservative. Under the CDA, don't bother trying to create a legally acceptable Web site that deals with issues like the prevention of rape or the spread of AIDS or other serious issues. Under the CDA, this essay is probably illegal to post on the net (because later I use the word "pissed").

Perhaps most importantly, the global nature of the Internet and the technology of which it is constructed makes it impossible for a U.S. law regarding content to have much useful effect. Any "objectionable" material will still be on servers in Amsterdam and elsewhere, still available to anyone in the world. (An interesting aside is that various projects undertaken on the net provide the full text of books banned anywhere in the world, so they are available everywhere in the world.) Thus, the CDA can't possibly have its intended effect of eliminating material from the net. While it can serve to repress what U.S. citizens say on the net, it can't repress what they read on the net.

The battle against the CDA has been waged by an overwhelming collection of common citizens, corporations and experts against a small number of radical right-wing kooks and a misguided Congress. Some of the plaintiffs in the lawsuits seeking to overturn the act include: the American Library Association; the American Society of Newspaper Editors; America Online, Inc.; American Booksellers Association, Inc.; American Civil Liberties Union; Apple Computer, Inc.; Association of American Publishers, Inc.; CompuServe Incorporated; Electronic Frontier Foundation; Health Sciences Libraries Consortium; Magazine Publishers of America, Inc.; Microsoft Corporation; National Press Photographers Association; Newspaper Association of America; Planned Parenthood; Prodigy Services Company; the Society of Professional Journalists; and the Citizens Internet Empowerment Coalition, representing nearly 50,000 individual Internet users.

This June, a Philadelphia federal appeals court struck down the CDA, saying in part, "Just as the strength of the Internet is chaos, so the strength of our liberty depends upon the chaos and cacophony of the unfettered speech the First Amendment protects.... As the most participatory form of mass speech yet developed, the Internet deserves the highest protection from government intrusion." A second federal appeals court (in New York) came to similar conclusions soon after. Those decisions are being appealed by the government to the U.S. Supreme Court, so this particular fight is not yet over. Even if we prevail here, we must always be ready to defend our rights. There will always be those who think their morality should be forced on the rest of us by the government.

But What Does Senator Exon Have To Do with Erotica?

Senator Exon (and the other sponsors of the bill that became the CDA) played a very important role in the publication of this book. They found it a publisher.

From the first time I heard about the bill that would become the CDA, I helped the fight in whatever small ways I could. Since I'd been a net citizen for ten years, the CDA wasn't just an abstract injustice for me to object to; it very directly threatened my personal civil liberties and my professional livelihood. I was pissed.

I was already a member of organizations that would lead the fight against the act (the Electronic Frontier Foundation and the Computer Professionals for Social Responsibility), I later joined the Citizens Internet Empowerment Coalition (thus adding my name to the list of plaintiffs in the legal case against the CDA) and I signed whatever petitions and letters I could to add my dissenting voice to the messages heard by our lawmakers.

Naturally, I followed the fight against the CDA by reading on the Web. During one session, I followed a link labeled "Why I Write Erotica." I liked the essay I read there. I strongly agreed with most of the ideas it expressed. I went on to read several other things by the same author, Mary Anne Mohanraj. Her writing was clear and powerful. I read that she was looking for a publisher for an anthology of her work. My first thought was "I'm a publisher, but my company doesn't publish that kind of stuff."

As I thought about it more, I realized that it was actually a good fit for IAM and that it was something I really wanted to do. I'd started my company as a more socially responsible place to work (a place where the human bottom line was just as important as this quarter's financials), and I had a chance to make good on that goal in several ways. The CDA stunk, and what better (or more ironic) way to protest it than by publishing "dirty stories" found on the Internet while giving full credit to Senator Exon and friends. Besides, Mary Anne already had a strong following of Internet fans, and IAM had one of the first commercial Web sites accepting orders via online forms (before there was even a company named "Netscape"). So we'd be in a good position to market the book to that waiting Internet audience.

Most importantly, Mary Anne isn't just any writer of erotica.

She uses erotica as a tool rather than as a means unto itself. As an author, she wants us to consider deeply the intellectual, philosophical, and ethical problems of our world. Some of those problems have to do with our own personal sex lives, or about what we tolerate in other people's sex lives. Other problems can still be examined metaphorically in erotic work. How better to bring them to our attention? Mary Anne's writing is certainly not only "literature designed to be read with one hand." It is stimulating and exciting, intellectually and otherwise.

Though I decided to go ahead and publish the book, I still had some reservations. I thought "maybe this or that is over the line, and maybe we ought to cut it." After talking with Mary Anne about it, and after thinking about it more, I realized the importance of keeping her work completely intact.

If I wanted to draw a line, where would I draw it? Ernest Hemingway once submitted a piece to the editor of *Esquire* with a letter that said "Here is the piece. If you can't say fornicate can you say copulate or if not that can you say co-habit? If not that would have to say consummate I suppose. Use your own good taste and judgment." I wanted the reader to have a strong impression of Mary Anne's vision, without the dilution of heavy-handed editing.

I found a new appreciation of how important and relevant art is in today's world, characterized this summer by the jumbo-jet which fell to the ocean without explanation, and a pipe-bomb exploded at the Olympics. We need desperately to drop old prejudices and to see new alternatives. We're comfortable with our usual perspective, and different views are sometimes uncomfortable.

Art that never disturbs us rarely moves us. We need to be moved.

Dale L. Larson,
Intangible Assets Manufacturing
dale@iam.com
http://www.iam.com

For more information on free speech and electronic civil liberties, see:
http://www.eff.org —Electronic Frontier Foundation
http://www.well.com/user/freedom/index.html
—Feminists for Free Expression
http://rainbow.rmii.com/~fagin/faic/
—Families Against Internet Censorship
http://www.cs.cmu.edu/~spok/banned-books.html
—Banned Books Online

TRACY LEE'S NOTES

I am an artist. I am afflicted.

Somewhere along my strands of DNA lies a particular combination of chemicals that make this so: I can no sooner change it (as if I would ever want to) than I could change my height or eye color or the shape of my face or the sound of my voice. It is hardwired in my genes. It is who I am, it is who I will always be.

I celebrate the human form in my art. My chosen tool is a camera, my laboratory is my studio and darkroom. I experiment with light and shadows, form and figure, grain and texture. For the past ten years I have been focusing my lens on exposing the human body—particularly the female body (specifically my female body).

I am an artist and I am happy in the dark.

Because of this I think a little differently than most others. I look at the world through the eyes of an artist. It's not better, it's not worse: it's just different. I am different. I am an artist and I am not the norm.

I forget this, and it gets me into trouble.

Personally I strive to be open-minded, I seek out what is shocking and against the grain. I observe, I immerse myself, I learn and I grow. What was shocking now becomes accepted and understood.

Nudity is an accepted part of my life. I look at a nude and I see beauty, I see the fluid motion, I see shapes and lines and forms. Looking at the work of others who share my love of the subject I see the emotion the artist wanted to convey, I experience the piece through the eyes of the photographer. There is beauty in the body. Every line, every curve. Faces sometimes don't matter: my photographs aren't about me (not always, anyway) but about a woman. Any woman. Look at her: what do you see? What do you feel?

I am proud of my work and I don't hide it away. This is what I do, this is who I am.

Not everyone feels the same as I do, not everyone agrees with my art, not everyone approves of my subject matter. A large percentage of the population seems to have forgotten that underneath all those layers they are just as naked as I am.

Every preacher who has ever spouted out against the evils of the flesh is naked up there on that pulpit. The members of Congress, the Supreme Court and the House of Representatives are all naked under their suits, dresses and robes. Senator Exon is naked. And though I can't be certain of this, Jesse Helms is probably naked too.

We are flesh and blood, bones and cartilage, sinew and muscle. We live, we breathe, we sweat and cry, we hope and dream. Unique as each individual personality might be, it all boils down to just how similar we all are on the basic level.

When Congress tries to pass laws censoring free speech I am confident in the fact that such a law can never be accepted because I know it's absurd. And so everyone must know it's absurd, right? But as person after person stands up and rails against the arts and the Internet and free speech and pornography and the poisoning of the minds of the children, I become very scared.

I'm not doing anything wrong, why are you persecuting me?

I firmly believe that an individual should just turn off the TV if something offends. There is a little knob right there on that radio dial and you can very well make that offensive music go away. You disagree with an art exhibition? Fine, don't support it, send your check somewhere else. You think that book is pornographic? I have a very easy answer: don't buy it.

But don't ban it, don't propose new legislation to rid the airwaves of it altogether, to prosecute publishers who produce works you think are indecent, to jail artists who create "pornography." I am a responsible adult and I voluntarily took on the job of raising my child when I gave birth. It angers and infuriates me that I am being second guessed by some old guy in a suit in DC who knows nothing about me at all. If something bothers you then stay away from it. But have the common decency to believe that I am an intelligent being who can think for myself and who is very capable of making her own decisions, thank you very much.

Where will this book reside in your home? Will you keep it out on the coffee table or will you hide it away in a drawer? Will you put it up high on the shelves away from prying eyes or will you read it openly in the middle of your family room? If your child saw you reading it would you quickly close the book and hide the cover or would you continue on? I am not saying that any of those things are bad, I just want you to think about why you would do it.

What message is society sending to the children when violence is glorified in movies and TV but sex is something forbidden and dirty?

Sex is a wonderful, beautiful thing and to deny this to yourself and to anyone is a waste. To embrace the beauty of sex is enlightening. Live, love, and enjoy. Human beings are created to have sex—it is as natural a part of life as living and breathing. Open your eyes, try something new, do something different. You're dead for a very long time, so don't throw away what time you have.

There is nothing wrong with being naked. And there is nothing really wrong with being disturbed or offended by it. But there is everything wrong with judging me and censoring my thoughts and ideas because they do not conform to your own.

I am artist. I want to make you think. If only for a moment, I want you to look at the world through my eyes. I want you to feel what I feel when I create it. And I want you see the beauty of the body.

I will keep trying.

Tracy Lee
Washington, D.C., October, 1996
tracylee@iam.com

MARY ANNE'S INTRODUCTION

People are fascinated by sex. It's a fact that can't be denied, however much the Moral Majority might like to. We see this daily, in the tools of the ad-men, in the whispers of the gossips, in the schoolboys sneaking looks at Playboy after school. This isn't a bad thing, in and of itself. Without sex, we wouldn't be around very long—doesn't it seem reasonable that we would take interest in such an innate biological drive?

What's interesting is that we choose to create a taboo about sex. No matter to what corner of the globe you venture, every culture has raised some proscriptions against sex. Often they contradict each other. The effect is to make sex even more desirable, since humans yearn for the forbidden, the taboo. So every senator thundering against the proliferation of smut on the Internet sends fifty or five hundred rushing out to get net accounts. Sex is a joyous and important act, and the discourse surrounding it can be a powerful tool. And what have we done with that tool? We've neglected it, and worse—we've left it in the hands of those who use it irresponsibly.

I'm talking partly about the moralists; the scared ones. The ones who point to sexuality as the cause of every ill on this earth, and preach that the only cure is absolute abstinence, or fidelity within a state-sanctified marriage. The ones who see every loving act as a crime against women, or against children, and so play on our fears till we feel slime in every caress and see a monster in every man. That's ridiculous and unfair, and gives far too little credit to our own ability to discriminate between danger and delight. We raise our daughters with fear rather than strength—then throw the blame on sex.

I'm also talking about men. Don't get me wrong—I'm very fond of men, and this isn't meant as some mass condemnation. But for far too long, men have had far more freedom to be really sexual beings than women have (though men have been repressed by society in different ways). Men have possessed more freedom to think about sex, to talk about it, to do it, while too many women have been ashamed of their sexuality. Even the most liberated man may contribute to the problem. I can't count the number of times I've met one of my readers—who then recoils, startled. "You mean you're really a woman?" They're then too embarrassed to even speak to me. I've turned from a fantasy or a delusion into a real breathing woman—one who discusses sexuality openly, and that's a creature that simply can't exist in their world-view. That's not their fault—it's the fault of a society which has dictated that 'good' women, 'nice' women, don't discuss sex. At least not in front of the menfolk. And so public sexuality has been left in the hands of the men, especially those men willing to exploit its vast potential.

I'm talking about the porn industry, which makes millions cranking out garbage. By garbage, I don't mean sex-related material—I mean sex-related material done badly, with no thought for portraying realistic people or emotions. Not to say that all porn needs to be sophisticated, subtle and elegant; I certainly think there's a place for writing that's simply fast and hot and maybe even a little cheesy. Neither need it all be factual; you'll see more than a few magical characters in my stories, and I think fiction would be poorer without that option. What I do object to are those unrealistic aspects that are damaging. For example, there are far too many stories where a woman is gang-raped, bleeding badly and still orgasming wildly. That's a frighteningly dangerous myth to be spreading. Or to take a less extreme example, too many porn-makers seem to think that a woman must have huge firm breasts to be sexy, or that men must have foot-long penises. Real people are sexy—people who sweat and swear and have sweet sagging breasts and get tired once in a while. A man isn't a machine, after all, and a reader who expects real life sex to be like the porn mags is in for a shock. I think it's long past time for intelligent thoughtful people to turn their energies in this direction—to use and shape this field to do something worthwhile. That's what I'm trying to do (along with quite a few others of course, but not enough—not nearly enough).

I'm fascinated by people, in all their strengths and weaknesses, and to my mind, nothing illustrates a person more effectively than how and what he or she loves. I attempt to use the vast power and majesty of sex to show the secrets of the human heart... and I admit to being an idealist. I want to change the world and make it a better place. I feel that human sexuality has been twisted for a long time. In my opinion, our culture (American culture is what I know, but I think it applies to most of the world) has an unhealthy fear of sexuality. We punish people for enjoying sex, for celebrating sex, for having sex with people of the wrong religion, race, gender, or even having the wrong kind of sex. I think that leads to people being unwilling or unable to talk about sex, and that leads to miscommunication and heartbreak. Take the problem of date rape alone—I wonder how many of those situations would have even come up in a society where sexuality was openly discussed and appreciated.

So I write these stories as part of my own attempt to change the world. I write stories with strong consenting women, to remind people that strong women are sexy and that consent is crucial. I write stories with characters of various sexual orientations and genders, to spread a little awareness. I write stories dealing with taboo subjects. Mainly, I try to write stories with real people—people who love and hate and fear and sometimes have sex for all the wrong reasons; people who have lives and hopes and dreams beyond the immediate sex act. I'm trying to shape a healthier world—a lofty goal, but I have help. Writers, publishers, the ACLU, reasonable people in government (few and far between, but they do exist).

You readers are the most important—you're willing to read my words; that's a big step. So there's my rant, and I leave you with instructions:

> Have safe, sane, consensual sex (or don't)
> with whomever you choose, however you choose…
>
> Fight for the right to do so and the right
> of everyone else to do so…
>
> Fight for the right to talk about it,
> or they'll take that right away from us too…
>
> And perhaps most importantly, spread the word.
> Silence is the great death.

Mary Anne Mohanraj
San Francisco, October, 1996
maryanne@iam.com
http://www.iam.com/maryanne/

WAS IT GOOD FOR YOU?

His hands press smooth against her waist as he guides her into the frantic club. The blast of heat and music hits them both. Now they are past the bouncers and the ticket counter, skimming past the teens in their translucent skirts and carefully bored expressions, down the stairs to the over-21 hangout, where he promises her interesting conversation and air-conditioning. Once there, pulled into a booth by his over-friendly friends, he curves her body to his and loosely links his hands around her waist. His thumbs etch small, slow circles on her belly through the thin black tank. She wonders if he remembers that she is seeing someone else. She wonders if he cares.

***

My first fumblings took place in my parents' finished basement, age fifteen. A neighbor boy and I sat cross-legged, facing each other beneath the staircase. When he asked if he could kiss me, I was so flattered that I said yes at once, though I actually had dreamed of his older brother. This kiss was not quite what I'd expected—damp and squishy, rather than exhilarating. His rough hands groped eagerly through my shirt, gently mauling my breasts. After a bit more groping, he pulled my hand to his crotch and asked me to rub. I pulled away, but offered to remove my shirt instead. He agreed this would be a fair exchange. When shirt and bra were removed, he bent to suck my nipples and I wondered, "Is this all?" An unpleasant week after, I manufactured an imaginary boyfriend to rescue me. That was the end to my sexual exploration for the next two years.

***

His hands move to her back, at first a gentle rub that no jealous lover could have protested, had one been there to see it. Fingers slide along the curve of scapula and spine, rise to caress her neck and rub tense shoulders, and butterfly-dance along stretches of bare skin. Palms press heavy against knots of tension, slow circlings. Fingers rise again to slide through her heavy weight of hair and rest against her scalp. In one swift movement he clenches his hands in her hair, pulling her taut against him, breath warm against her neck… then, with a laugh, releases her. She laughs too, shivers racing through her, muscles clenched. The conversation swirls around them.

***

In college, I met a man. We had absolutely nothing in common, but those sparks so conspicuously absent two years before were flaring high. Fucking in private and semi-public, on soft beds and concrete floors, to the dismay of roommates and the abandonment of dignity. I was even a little in love, as was he. For a while. When the sparks died for him, they still raged in me, and I pursued him for far too long. When he finally acquiesced, it was swift and joyless, in a place and time not of my choosing and in a manner that brought pleasure to neither of us. It did have the salutary effect of killing any last thoughts of salvaging the relationship.

***

Impatient with this slow seduction, he stands, pulling her up with him. They move upstairs again, to the dance floor which at this hour has become a solid mass; a slowly writhing, sweaty black void. They insinuate themselves into the creature, pressed close by necessity. Her groin is tight within her, a twisted heat radiating to her skin, to each cell that lays against his slickness. She makes no resistance when he grinds against her, palms tight against her hips. Eyes closed, she moves as he wills her. One of his thighs slides between hers, and she lifts one leg to wrap around his hip. Thus locked, one of his hands is free to slip up her body, beneath the tank to cup and caress her breasts. They have long since crossed the forbidden line, and now she wonders if there is any point to resisting further. He bends to run teeth along her neck and she shudders, biting back a moan.

***

Years later, I lived with a man I loved. The sex had always been good, occasionally great, and the conversation was better. There were times when he could bring me to the point of coming with a kiss, or a whispered promise. So how could I protest those few times when his interest outstripped my own, when I would rather have curled up with a good book and a mug of cocoa? He was unfailingly gentle, always patient, so what harm could there be in simulating more pleasure than I actually felt? The emotion was there, after all. I wanted to please him… pleasing him pleased me. I convinced myself that that was enough.

***

They leave the club, his arm firm around her shoulder. Driving home, his hand roams across her body, but exhaustion rises in her now, and she merely simulates response. In her apartment, he strips confidently, knowing that she will not back out now. He is sure in his ability to please her, and assiduous in his attentions to her needs. His mouth travels the paths his fingers had patterned in the club before, and when he slides within her, she is wet. He holds off his own climax, waiting for hers, and under his gentle, unwavering assault, she surrenders, and moans for him.

JINSONG

Date: Fri, 15 May 1994
From: dancer@cs.pdx.edu (Matthew Danzener)
To: wan9@midway.uchicago.edu (Jinsong)
Subject: Re: your last poem...

You probably don't remember me; I wrote you a while ago asking you
about a Yeats poem you quoted...

I just wanted to say how much I...umm...enjoyed your last poem. I
was pretty stunned, actually. While I've been following your work
for a while, and you've certainly had your high points and low
points, I was really impressed with your honesty here.

I'm enclosing a copy below, just so you know which one I mean. I
wrote you one in response - if you like, I'll send it to you...

   - Matthew

* * * * *

Confession

> (You ask what I want.
> I cannot tell you: Catholic upbringing, New England prudery,
> a habit of silence combine to smother the words.
> So write it, you say.)

I want everything, you see.
Men and women
indoors and out
top and bottom and sideways
to come screaming in a deserted forest
so that the only creatures startled are the deer.

More than a little bit of an exhibitionist.

Eyes watching
caressing
stripping away the layers
the flimsy chiffon covering of propriety
leaving me gloriously naked to a stranger's fevered gaze.

I tease them shamelessly walking down the street
in cut-off jeans and minimal tank, hair swinging.

I make them wonder as they read my words
stare at the screen
touch themselves

> (wonder if this is me; wonder if it is only a poem).

Riding the power trip
to its heights

> (and I will taste the depths)

tied down so all I can do is strain against the black silk
blindfolded, so I don't know whether you will lick a nipple next
spank me until I'm sore and screaming
begging for more.

I am not quite as brave as I would wish, but if I could

> I would risk getting caught on the quads at night.
> I would have two men at once, maybe three.
> I would be fucked until I pass out.
> I would have sex with someone without knowing whom it is.
> I would do all the shameful things a good Catholic girl
>   should never, ever think of.

And I would tell you about it.

Date: Fri, 15 May 1994
From: wan9@midway.uchicago.edu (Jinsong)
To: dancer@cs.pdx.edu (Matthew Danzener)
Subject: Re: your last poem...

Thanks for writing, I'm glad you enjoyed it.

And sure, send me the one you wrote...I'm curious now. It's been a
very long time since anyone's written me a poem.

  - Jinsong

What - You don't have lovers writing you poems daily? That's hard to
believe... If I were in Chicago, you'd get roses and poems on your
doorstep every day.

Here's the poem. (Since you asked...)

Please
Please don't be offended
if I also say something hard
hard to say
what's on my mind
what's on every
one's mind
Please
meet me
in the dark
in a room
at midnight
or on the Sears Tower
observation deck
at noon
and we will
and I will
and you will
and then...
I can't say it
because you might be offended
but it would have been
spectacular.
(What I wanted to say,
but don't have the nerve,
was that I would
like
to
fuck you
to absolution...
But I am too shy to say this
to anyone I don't know,
and also
to anyone I do know,
so I'm not saying it to you,
and it remains thought

but unsaid, and I hope
you remain
unoffended...)

Matthew Danzener

I'm a little stunned. That's certainly the best wanna fuck I've ever
gotten. I might cry. I can't really speak - and that's impressive,
stealing away a poet's words.

Thank you.

 - Jinsong

Hey, I really didn't mean to make you cry. I just wanted to give you
something in return, after that seductive image of your bare thighs,
and hair swinging loose against the small of your back. I could
almost taste the sweat collecting on the base of your neck, under
all that gorgeous hair.

Sorry, you probably don't even have long hair. Ok, I admit it!
I'm insanely curious about whether you have long black hair.
Or blue eyes. Or dry gold skin. Or wicked nails, to rake a lover's
back...

Are you a romantic? I want to take you to the 95th Floor in Chicago
for brunch, then walk along Wacker Drive and watch the sparkle on
the river. I want to take you to the beach at night and walk across
the jagged rocks, somewhere we can see the city skyline, and kiss
you till you're dizzy and only my arms keep you from falling.

I want to take you.

At least you don't sound offended... Yet(?)

Matthew

I'm not offended. Flattered, really - I've had a hard couple of
weeks - just broke up with my boyfriend, after an angstful relationship over the last year, and it's nice to get some attention.

And yes, I'm a romantic. An utter, hopeless romantic. But I hate
mush and sticky sentiment. Can you walk that line?

I'm demanding in my lovers. I want sweetness and sexiness, strength
and vulnerability. I want a woman who can make me come just by
spanking me, and a man who trembles when I kiss the small of his
back. And the reverse, of course. I want utter honesty...but I admit
that I play games sometimes. And compliments embarrass me. And I'm
sometimes more brave than wise.

So a description - I'm small, slightly plump. Straight black hair,

pale skin that oddly doesn't seem to burn. Green eyes...my mother is
gorgeous, but that's unfortunately the only feature I seem to have
gotten from her. I'm really my father's daughter. He's a professor
in Near Eastern Studies here at U Chicago. Where are you, anyway?
And what do you look like?

Who are you?

  - Jinsong

I'm sorry about your boyfriend...at least, I'm sorry you're sad...
but honestly, you sound beautiful! And your openness and honesty
makes you so very appealing. It's hard to believe you're so far
away. If you were here...or I was there...

As for me... skinny, strong, not too tall, scraggly brown hair with
a winter-only beard, blue eyes, semi-introverted,
but with a charming smile.

I'm in Pennsylvania...but I spent a summer in Chicago once. And
would like to go back again. Maybe this summer?

Promise not to be offended if I tell you what I really want?

Matthew

No promises. Be brave.

  - Jinsong

I'd like to pick you up
pick you up
at your place
in my rental car
you've been sad
So I hug you tight
steal a quick kiss
and here's a rose
we'll go out
to dinner
we'll go to your favorite spot
and have a glass of wine
we'll get wine-happy together
laughing and talking
the waiter has to come back
we forgot to look at the menus
then under the table
I rub the back
of your hand with mine
and then off
onto your thigh
with my nervous hand

```
I hope you don't mind.
I am becoming intoxicated
with your presence.
So many thoughts I have
you and I
this way and that,
here and there
but I can't tell you
these thoughts
they aren't decent.
You smile at me
at my awkward boyish attempts
After dinner
I want to take you
to a movie
we can walk from here
it's close
hand in hand
I lust for your touch
in everyway
We'll sit in the back row
(because this is my fantasy)
no one joins us
and in the darkness
my arm around your shoulder
I kiss you
and take your hand
slowly
onto my leg
and you rub my thigh
gently up and down
higher next time
and then higher still
and my intoxication
of you
reaches new heights
I am so drunk
on you
that nothing else matters
and your hand brushes against
my crotch
and the world disappears
and only you and I exist
for the moment
and I kiss you on the forehead
and moan softly in your ear
to show you
how much
how so very much
and you smile at me again
in the movie sound, soft-lit
theatre darkness
and you rub more firmly now
you are pleased
my spare hand has found your breast
under your jacket
```

and I caress gently first
until I feel the nipple
rising up peakedly
and I focus more on it
as you work your magic on me.
No one is near us
in this back row
so you move deftly
in a defiance of all that
is proper
and you unzip my pants
and reach in
and it is all I can do now
to control myself
to not scream out
at the pleasure
that's mine
that you are giving
with your hand as
my cock spasms in your grasp
with a throbbing aching need,
in a way I can only remember
it doing when I was
in my teens and
every girl was
wickedly unavailable.
I move my breast hand down
down across your uncharted mids
to your netherworld
to your sacredness
to your promised land
of milk and honey
to your zippered crotch
and you spread
just a bit
for my hand to penetrate
to your jeans covered warmth
your covered secrets
and I rub you
gently first
until you press against my hand
and squeeze my cock pulsingly
as if to signal your approval
(since this is my fantasy)
you look around
furtively
and there is no one else
seated nearby
it's a darkish movie
so you slide quietly
down to the floor
on your knees facing
and over in front of me
you are small
you barely fit
but a certain duty

calls
and you honor it
as you take my throbbing hardness
in your mouth
your warm wet mouth
your delicate lipped
eager, inquisitive mouth
and you tease me
with your slowness
as I want impatiently
to give you everything
to give up my reality
in exchange for this moment
this surreal moment
when nothing matters
except this act
this strange act of sex
of love, of total selfless giving
of yourself
to my need
And you suck me
succinctly
exquisitely
hungrily
up and down...

I have so many more fantasies, but I am afraid. Afraid of letting
go, afraid of being the real me, and offending you with the real me,
instead of this facade that I march behind in my normal daily life.
No one else who knows me would think that I wrote the above.

Can I come see you this summer? School will be over in a few weeks
and plane tickets aren't that expensive.
Matthew

I'm blushing, and crying, and excited all at once. The crotch of my
jeans is uncomfortably tight, and the person sitting next to me just
glanced at the screen, and glanced quickly away.

To have a stranger offer all this...is exciting. And frightening.
But even more exciting, I think.

If you wouldn't mind my roommate and her boyfriend coming along at
first (we can always ditch them later)...then yes. YES.

Come to Chicago. Come touch me, come taste me, buy me roses and
don't be upset if they fall in the street while I'm kissing you. Let
me shred your clothing, and your back - I will sharpen my nails and
paint them gold for you.

I've been so very lonely.

 - Jinsong

I want to ask you to promise something...but I won't. You don't seem
to like promises.

Instead, I'll tell you what I hope.

I hope that I am who you think I am...and you are who I think you
are.
I hope that we like each other...that we become friends.
I hope that the summer heat will help us drop inhibitions.
I hope that we have sex on the quads.
I hope you like the way I taste.

and...

I even hope that maybe this might last a little longer than a summer
fling. That maybe you could learn to care for me. I think I'm
already learning to care for you. (enough. I'm afraid I've already
gotten too sentimental for your tastes. I'm afraid.)

I bought the tickets today. I'll be there in two weeks.

Matthew

Oh, I don't know how to say this. Once again, Matthew, I'm without
words.

I'm sorry. What an empty, useless phrase. However true it may be.

My boyfriend and I got back together last night. Whether this is
wise, I don't know...but I do know that now it would be impossible
for me to see you. Or to touch you. Honestly, I didn't even want to
write this...funny how much cowardice hides inside.

You're a sweet, wonderful guy. I'm sure if you keep looking, you'll
find somebody less fucked-up than I am.

Thank you for holding me up when I was drowning.

Don't write back, please.

  - Jinsong

MEMORY TEARS UPON
CLOSE EXAMINATION

You see, I did not want
to take refuge in
simple description:

> yellow-gold hair
> glass-blue eyes
> and palm-filling breasts.

I treasured instead
the crease down her belly;
the snake-curve of her back;
her almost-silence as we slid
together, that betraying gasp
muffled against sodden skin…

and oh
god,
I have already forgotten the rest.

SEASON OF MARRIAGE

She was dizzy with the smoke. The traditional wedding had lasted almost three hours, and the heat and oil fumes from the ever-present lamps had combined to make Raji feel slightly queasy. And the chanting. It went on and on and on in Sanskrit incomprehensible to a girl who'd grown up with a New England accent. She was suddenly homesick—for America, for Connecticut, for forests and hills and snow and people you didn't have to watch every word around for fear of treading on some custom you didn't understand. Despite the cold and pain that had driven her to this wedding in the baking heat of New Delhi, Connecticut was home. And it was much, much too late to go back. She was married. The wedding reception was ending now, and it would soon be time to leave with this kind-seeming stranger, to go to the house of his mother (whom Raji already despised), to go to his bed. And all her American casualness about sex, the casualness and experience she had counted on to see her through this ordeal, suddenly was meaningless. She was scared. Why, oh why had she agreed to this?

The answer to that was easy. Because she hadn't cared anymore. After she'd found out about Jim and that other girl; after all the broken promises and shattered dreams, it just didn't seem to matter. The heat and incense combined to bring on a wave of brutally clear memory.

***

They'd just collapsed, Jim on top of her, as he always insisted. He was crushing her with his weight... not fat of course, but muscle was even heavier. Raji managed to roll to the side, and then turned to gaze adoringly into his eyes, still amazed that this gorgeous man would really want her.

"You were wonderful."

"Uh huh." He was still panting, but in a very sexy way, she thought.

"Jim?"

"Uh huh."

"I love you."

There was a disconcerting pause. Before he'd always responded, "I love you, too." Now, he said nothing, and looked almost... guilty?

"Ummm..."

"Yes?" she asked, eagerly.

"I should probably tell you something. Now don't get too upset, okay?"

And he proceeded to tell her about Sharmila. Also Indian. Two years older. Drop-dead gorgeous with unfairly huge breasts. Who he'd been sleeping with for three weeks. His conscience had finally kicked in. Or maybe he was just bored with Raji, and this was the easiest way to make her break up with him. Which she, of course, did.

***

Looking back, she knew it was the right decision… but it had sunk her into a black fit of depression where she had let everyone else make decisions for her. She'd decided that maybe her parents were right, after all. Maybe American men really were slime. Maybe she'd be happiest with someone like herself. So she'd agreed to meet some Indian men, and the next thing she knew she was flying to India to meet this man Vivek. And he was gentle. And kind. Rich and generous; he'd bought her a pearl necklace the day after they met. And though she'd only known him for a few days her parents thought he was very suitable and his parents liked her and it was suddenly all arranged and they were asking her and she said yes.

And now she was suddenly remembering all the sweet guys she'd grown up with and wondering where they'd gone. She was finally shaking off the depression that had lasted the four months since Jim and just knew that she'd have been happier with an American she understood rather than with this stranger from a strange land that she'd left when she was three. And it was still too late. She was married, and though she could probably get a divorce, Raji wasn't the sort to give up on anything that easily. And it would break her mother's heart. Her dear, scheming, conniving, thoroughly manipulative mother. Sometimes Raji couldn't figure out whether she loved or hated her.

Her silence was noted by Vivek, who asked her in perfect, if heavily accented English, if she felt all right. Raji nodded, then stood with him as the interminable reception finally came to a close. Her legs were trembling, she realized, as she wondered what this almost certainly virgin man would think of a very experienced American. She'd find out soon enough.

The women took her to the bedroom and helped her undress, giving her fragments of advice in broken English as they helped her into a flowing white nightgown, incredibly demure and perfectly opaque. Raji barely heard them, caught somewhere between tears and laughter. She waited patiently, allowing them to dress her as they chose and lead her toward the crimson-draped bed. One woman, who Raji thought was her new sister-in-law and recently married herself, touched Raji's shoulder before she left, pityingly. Then they were gone.

Vivek appeared, ghost-like in the doorway, dressed in flowing white to match her. He walked toward her silently; a hunter afraid of startling some strange, wild creature he had never before seen. Raji was determined to try her best, and so smiled, slightly trembling. Vivek returned her smile with a tentative smile of his own, and, standing before her now, reached his hand up to touch her cheek. His hand was not damp and sweaty as she had somehow feared, but warm and dry, as if lit by some inner fire. He had not touched her before this, in all the days of wedding preparations during the short month since they had met. Even when placing the gold thali wedding necklace around her neck, he had taken care not to touch her. She was suddenly grateful for his gentleness, and stepping boldly towards him, stretched her slim brown arms to encircle his thick neck, surprised to find that he was shaking too. Vivek was not very handsome, but sturdily built, with hair thicker and richer than her own and deep brown eyes. Raji had thought them dull and calf-like before, but suddenly she was not so sure. There was a hint of laughter in those eyes, and a sparkle of what might possibly be intelligence. Of course, he was a doctor (nothing else would have satisfied her mother) and so couldn't be entirely stupid. Now, with her hands locked behind his neck and her delicate body inches away from his, Raji found herself bemused, not sure what to do next, or how fast she should take this. He solved that problem for her.

He placed his arms around her waist, gently. Tilting his head, he kissed her. She was startled, not at being kissed, but at being kissed by him, and stiffened in his arms. He raised his head questioningly.

"Is this not customary in America?"

"Yes, yes it is. I didn't think it was here."

"We are not as ignorant as you Americans assume. We do watch movies, after all."

Now Raji was sure that he was laughing at her, as he leaned down to kiss her again. Despite his claims to knowledge she was fairly sure that kissing was new to him, and so responded gently to the firm pressure on her lips. They kissed chastely for long minutes, until Raji, greatly daring, opened her mouth and touched her tongue to his lips. He broke away for a moment, plainly startled, but then returned to kissing her with enthusiasm, opening his own mouth and tasting her lips, her teeth, her tongue with his own. She tilted her head backwards, hoping he would get the hint, and he did - kissing her cheek, her nose, her ear, tracing a delicate line along her cheekbone with his tongue. He went slowly, seemingly enchanted with the wonder of it all, and Raji stood still, eyes closed, feeling him touch her so gently. This was new to her—this gentleness, this seeming reverence. She had enjoyed sex with Jim, but it had always been hard and fast, a summer storm - quickly started, quickly over. Vivek was twenty-five, years older than Jim had been, but he smiled with the wonder of a child.

Continuing to explore her chocolate skin, he slid slowly down her neck, dropping kisses like raindrops to lie wetly, quivering with her breath. Raji continued to hold still, starting to wonder how long she could act the trembling virgin... how long it would be before her impatience broke through. His kisses were abruptly stopped by the laces at the top of the gown, and he froze and locked her eyes with his. Raji slowly reached up, and almost teasingly, pulled free the tangled white ribbons and laces. Vivek undid them completely, sliding the white fabric off her creamy brown shoulders, continuing the slow kisses that had fallen like cool rain but now began to burn. Despite a ceiling fan, the room was stiflingly hot to a woman bred to New England winters, and Raji began suddenly to sway, dizzy with heat and unexpected passion. Vivek caught and held her, as the gown slid from her bare body to pool on the green-tiled floor. Cradling her against him with one arm, he pulled aside mosquito netting and drapes with the other. Picking her up, he gently deposited Raji on the bed and pulled the sheet over her. All this happened so quickly that Raji had no moment in which to become frightened again in her nakedness, and then he was undressing too, undoing the wrap of white fabric and climbing in beside her, pulling the mosquito netting closed so that they might be undisturbed.

"Are you all right?" he asked.

"Yes, I think so. Are you?"

"Of course I am. I'm a man."

Laughter again, from both of them this time, which trailed away into silence. He looked suddenly vulnerable, Raji thought, as he sat there cross-legged on the wide bed. The silence grew more and more awkward until Raji finally raised herself a little on her elbows, letting the sheet fall down to bare her curving breasts and smiling, puckered her lips for a kiss. He laughed again, and suddenly he was swooping down on her in mid-laugh, slipping his broad hands around her fragile frame. Raji was startled before she began drowning in a hail of fierce kisses and caresses. His hands explored in the lamplit dimness what he could not see, curving to fit her small breasts, each of which fit into the palms of his hands. He fumbled a little, sometimes touching her too softly, sometimes too fiercely, but always kissing so she was blinded by the rain and arching into his touch.

Vivek slid his hands down her stomach, across her hips, gently pushing apart her trembling thighs. She stiffened suddenly, and opening her eyes wildly searched for his, until he, looking up, caught her trapped gaze.

"Don't be afraid." he reassured her, though his voice was trembling.

"I'm a doctor, it's all right."

"I'm not, it's just... there's something I need to tell you."

"Shhh... don't worry."

Vivek smiled at the confusion in her eyes, and leaned down to kiss her. At the moment he kissed her he entered her, and Raji was suddenly so hot, so wet and ready for him that she thought she might scream. But remembering his despised mother in the next bedroom, she buried the sound in her throat and only moaned, softly, curving up to meet him as he began long, hesitant strokes, stretching through her long-neglected body, giving it the attention it so desperately wanted.

The world blurred for Raji to a haze of cloudy netting above her, lit by the lamp glow and measured by the rhythmic movement of this man, her husband, inside her. Some time during that long eternity it began to rain outside their window, but the thunder and lightning couldn't begin to match the pleasure arcing through her. He began pounding faster and faster to match the storm, and came suddenly, and she was caught in a moment of purest frustration underneath him. She opened her eyes to see his concerned face above her.

"That didn't work very well, did it? I'm sorry."

"Shhh... it's fine," she reassured him. "We have lots of time to practice. But there's a couple of things I don't understand."

"So ask."

"Well, for one, why is it still raining? I thought storms in India were short."

"Usually they are, but this one will last a while. It's the beginning of monsoons, remember? It will be storming for the next three months."

"Oh."

Raji had the distinct feeling that he was laughing at her again. Vivek smiled brightly at her, rolling her towards him to rest in the crook of his arm. The storm raged more fiercely outside, churning the dirt paths to mud, soaking the very air.

"Want to ask one of the harder question now?"

"There's just one more. You know I'm not a virgin now. Do you mind?"

She closed her eyes and clenched her fists against the answer, suddenly wanting desperately to make this gentle man happy, especially happy with her.

"I knew from the beginning. Your mother seemed to feel I had a right to know what I was bargaining for."

"She told you? How could she? She didn't even know..." Raji was caught somewhere between anger and relief.

"You would be surprised what mothers know. Mine really isn't so bad; she's just not looking forward to my leaving with you."

"Leaving?" Raji was now completely confused.

"For America. Next week. Lots of work for doctors there, I hear. The problem in India is that everyone who can becomes a doctor. There aren't enough jobs. I've been hoping to live in America for a long time, and I could hardly expect my beautiful American wife to be like the innocent girls of the villages here."

"You're sure you don't mind?"

"I'm sure."

And suddenly Raji was free to acknowledge to herself just how much she longed for apple trees and miniskirts and rollercoasters. India had its own strange beauty, its passion and mystery, but she was an American at heart.

Vivek touched her cheek and said, "Shall we try that again? My mother will be very upset with me if you continue to be so quiet. She will think that I have been too rough with you and that you are crying." Raji held herself still for a moment, looking up at the face of her new husband. He was such a mass of surprises. Then suddenly she rolled over so that she was lying on top of him. Raji began kissing him wildly, ignoring his startled eyes. She stopped for a moment to tell him, "You're about to find out just how rough American women can be..." before she returned to teasing him unmercifully, rubbing her small breasts across his hairy chest. Vivek responded with renewed passion, pulling her close, and Raji finally left behind all thoughts of mothers and matchmaking, allowing herself to go spiraling downward with her husband.

Any sounds they made were soon drowned in the pounding of the monsoon storms.

(for Raji. I hope it was at least this good.)

MEDITATION ON HUMAN RELATIONS

...writing a sex scene at work because you just have to have an orgasm now or you'll die and there's nothing there to read and you can't get off without it, so you write it while you're rubbing your thighs together, and you rub the fabric of your long skirt that you've got shoved up under this desk where nobody can see it against your aching clit—no soft, pretty love scene, not when you're this horny, oh no, you know you want fast sex, rough sex, the way you think you'd like it, though you're ashamed to admit it and afraid to try it and you think you'd want someone to push you into it with him and a friend or maybe a couple at once—you might even want to try pulling a train, with your body out there and it's theirs and yours all at once and incandescent but you get a little anxious and so embarrassed to mention it, 'cause while it's all right nowadays for women to like sex, they're not supposed to like sex that looks like rape and they're not supposed to like sex that might be degrading, and they're especially not supposed to wonder if they might actually like rape after all—were it the right kind of rape, of course, the fantasy kind where you're so hot and dripping that nothing hurts, that nothing they do could damage you as you climb screaming up and over that edge—not like the real kind, where usually you're so dry that even a gentle one would hurt you and a real rapist rips you apart, and leaves you sobbing or too broken for tears. Who could do that? Maybe that's one of the fundamental problems between men and women, because I don't understand how you could keep taking your pleasure, despite knowing, and you must know, that you're tearing somebody apart underneath you. And maybe even taking some of that pleasure because of what you're doing to them. But then again, maybe it's not a fundamental difference, because come to think of it, I know plenty of women who do that too, just not in a physical sexual kind of way. People are fucked.

CHARLIE

Charlie's gone, with a hand to my cheek and a peck on my forehead, the sort I once found endearing, gone to play computer games and be paid for them, leaving me with five minutes. Five minutes in which to toss the egg-stained dishes in the dishwasher and shut the door, in which to grab a sponge from the sink and quickly unbutton my blouse, sponging off the summer sweat from underarms and under heavy breasts, five minutes until the knock on the back door. And I put down the sponge and open it, blouse seductively unbuttoned, knowing that Peter will have an excuse ready in case Charlie's running late today, "Hey, pal. I had to go downtown to pick up some paints—wondered if you wanted a ride in to work." And had the car pool been late, Charlie would have taken Peter up on it with a smile and a cheerful, unsuspecting "Thanks!" and a precious forty-two minutes would have been lost, one minute down the brownstone stairs, twenty minutes there, twenty minutes back, one minute up again.

But Charlie is gone, as he usually is, and so I am the one opening the door to Peter's cheerful smile, and with a quick fluttery glance at Kate and Alison's down the hall door, he slips inside and the door is shut and I am caught up in his arms, in his eyes, in him. Today he is hungry and the remaining buttons pop off the silk blouse, one two three and I note that I must find them later and sew them on and then his hands are pushing down the bra so my breasts spill out and his devouring mouth is on them. I must lean against the wall, hands braced flat, fingers down or I will fall. The fire sweeps through me fast, so fast and I have barely seen or touched or smelled him yet and yet the dampness is sliding from bare cunt to bare thighs. His hands, big, rough, incongruously broad for an artist's hands are around my waist now and lifting me up and onto him. The loose skirt is no impediment and I wrap legs around him, not bothering to wonder when he undid zippers and moved inconvenient clothing, just glad glad glad that it is gone and there is no obstruction between us.

Oh, dangerous we are being, as I ride him, tender breasts rubbing up and down against a heavy flannel shirt and muscled chest beneath, my mouth on his neck and my arms wrapped around him now, fingers digging red welts even through the shirt no doubt. No matter—he has no spouse to wonder at strange markings. Peter's kisses are gentle, always, no matter what the force of passion—he is too wise to leave visible marks. Not that Charlie could or would stand up to him, but this arrangement is convenient; it suits us all, even Charlie though he does not know it. I am hungry too, hungry for love and passion, and if Peter's whispered words are only a gentle illusion, no matter—it is enough. Let Charlie have his games and Peter his safe downstairs daily fuck and me my taste of danger and delight.

Peter's hands pull me to him roughly, and his muttered groans pull me over my own edge as I feel his come spilling into me and I dissolve.

Peter thinks that I am on the pill. But I would rejoice in a child if it came, and sometimes I think that if it did I would leave them both, my dear husband and my daring love, and even my ladder-climbing back-stabbing corporation. I would take her up into the mountains, and we would sit together by a lake and sing with the birds and I would never never never speak of love to her. Then the timer from the microwave beeps madly, and we are quickly kissing and he is out the door, and I rush through my ten minutes to shower and dress all over again before heading downtown, not forgetting to pick up the buttons and the blouse and needle and thread to take with me, so I can change before returning home, though Charlie will likely work late again tonight.

Mary Anne Mohanraj

TURNING BODIES

curled on blue stained comforter
your head on my thighs—I run short fingers
through white-gold

      silent, speak of men
      we have known
      love, we have imagined

digital glow reminds me
you must drive skidding soon through rain—
turn my body to shield your eyes

if only I didn't know what you'd do
if I kissed you
perhaps I'd kiss you
and see what you'd do.

PAINT

Paint fumes were thick in the sun-drenched room, and the clear wash of cream we were slapping on the walls did little to reflect the heat. Liza had propped the windows open with empty paint cans and pieces of wood when we came in to survey the damage, but that only let in hot July breezes. Andrew was covered in sweat already, his white t-shirt clinging to his lanky body. Liza and I, also in cut-offs and t-shirts, weren't much better off.

We'd let him do most of the heavy lifting involved in clearing out the apartment. Liza's father owned the building, and somehow she'd talked us into helping her make one of the apartments habitable again. A horde of college guys had trashed the place, leaving beer cans and mysterious stains everywhere, and then left with the summer.

"Can you pull the stepladder over here, Steph?" Liza asked. She'd somehow wedged her way up onto a windowsill to paint above it, and one of us had pulled the ladder away to work on something else. For a moment I was tempted to leave her crouched up there... but the thought passed. After all, Andrew would just lift her down.

I dragged over the stepladder and held it steady as she climbed down, her long, slightly furry legs descending past my upturned face. Liza nodded her thanks before walking over to where Andrew was painting large swirly stripes of cream on the battered wall. She laughed as he stood back to admire his artistry. He casually reached out and pulled her to him.

"What do you think? Would the Museum of Modern Art give me five thousand for it?" he asked.

"I think you should get back to work" Liza replied, digging her fingers into the ticklish spot under his bottommost right rib. He grabbed her fingers and pulled her hands behind him, laughing. She smiled up at him and he smiled down at her, and I couldn't watch anymore. I headed to the kitchen, calling out behind me, "Anyone else want something to drink?" They didn't respond.

As I downed some apple juice straight from the large bottle, I tried to figure out if there was a graceful way to get out of this situation and go home. It wasn't surprising that Andrew would spend a day of his vacation lugging battered sofas and futons around, since he'd come out here to visit her in any case, but what I was doing there was anyone's guess.

You'd think I'd have more sense than to spend time with those two. Liza and I had been best friends since second grade, and usually when I was home from college we spent lots of time together. I suppose it wasn't surprising that we were this summer too. But when Andrew had dumped me in April, I certainly hadn't expected that he'd take up with my best friend a month later.

To be fair, I don't think either of them expected it either. She came out to visit for a week... and it just sort of happened. Two lonely people, with at least one thing in common. That week Liza was there I hardly saw her. I'd catch glimpses of her, huddled in a shadowy stairwell with him, her arms locked around his neck. Or hear them talking softly outside my door before she came in to crash on my floor. There were times when I would have cheerfully, creatively, killed them both.

I put back the juice and turned back to the hall leading to the living room. As I trudged down the hall, Liza came towards me. She said, "I just realized that we need paint for the trim. I'm going to take the car and run get some. It should take about half an hour, I think. You don't mind if I leave you stranded, do you?"

"No, that's okay," I replied. "Is Andrew going with you?"

"I told him I expected him to have that room done when I got back," she laughed. "Keep an eye on him, all right?"

"Sure, chica," I said, as she walked past me and out the door.

When I entered the room, I noticed that Andrew's shirt lay discarded on the floor near one of the paint trays. His back and arms were slick with sweat, as he sent long, slow strokes along the edge of the far wall. I couldn't help staring, watching the muscles move under his skin, just wishing, for a second...

"Hey, Steph," he said, turning to face me. "Do I have to do this all alone?" His face was red and sweaty, and there was a distinct bulge at his crotch. I remembered then that Liza was still a virgin, and wanted to remain one. Perhaps I might have felt sympathy for him then, if I hadn't remembered their matching smiles.

Something twisted in me, and I couldn't help saying, "I think you could use a little loneliness for a change." I turned away, fighting unexpected tears, and picked up a brush and started to paint, slowly, calmly. Suddenly, Andrew's arms were around me, his left hand pressed against the skin at my waist, the right still holding a paintbrush in front of me. At the contact, the pressure of his long body against my back, I broke. Tears were suddenly pouring down my face. Weeks of pent-in frustration burst loose, and it was all I could do not to slam my paintbrush right through the newly-painted wall.

He just held me, quietly crooning an incomprehensible something, calming my shuddering body with the solidness of him. I calmed down eventually, turning in the circle of his arms to face him and wipe the tears from my cheeks with paint-daubed hands.

"It's all right," I said then. "You can let go now—I'll be fine."

The concern on his face shifted to something else at my words, and I suddenly caught my breath at what I thought I saw. "What if I don't want to let go?" he asked. Before I could answer his mouth was on mine, his tongue probing gently but with determination. The paintbrush in his hands dropped to the floor, and I couldn't help thinking, "We'll have to wipe that up" before his hands clenched my buttocks and pulled me to him.

We fell to the floor then, clothes somehow being unbuttoned and peeled off, mouths and fingers seeking skin they had barely touched in months. I buried my face in Andrew's shoulder, digging my teeth into his skin. He responded only by raking his fingers across my back, and I moaned, arching underneath him.

I barely noticed him scrounging around on the floor until he found his shorts, pulling a condom out of the pocket. His mouth was fastened to my breast as if he would never let go. He did, eventually, but only to slide up my slick body and into me, in a smooth remembered motion. The paint fumes grew stronger then, or I grew dizzy. We moved against the sanded wood floor, limbs locked, hearts racing. When I came, I came screaming. When he came, he was silent, as always.

We lay there naked for a while. My eyes were closed, and for a moment, with the weight of his body against me, I almost wanted to forget… The sweat on my back finally began to itch, and reaching back to scratch it, I found my fingers covered in paint. I let go of him and rolled away (he had already released me), turning to look beneath where I'd lain. Somewhere along the line we'd knocked over a paint tray, and the spreading pool had thoroughly coated my back and neck.

I swore and jumped up, grabbing for a rag to wipe up the mess. He sat up as well, watching silently as I knelt and mopped up the sticky paint. "Need help?" he finally offered, just as I was finishing. "No," I replied. "I think you've done enough."

He looked hurt at that, an injured puppy. "You were hardly fighting me," he pointed out.

"I know," I replied, as I pulled my clothes back on. A mess of emotions was roiling my stomach. "That's part of the problem." It was then that we heard the car pulling up. Looking out, I saw Liza stepping out, lugging two cans of paint. "It's Liza," I said. "You'd better get dressed."

I walked down the hall, leaving him naked behind me, frantically grabbing up clothes. I met her on the stairway.

"Could you give me a ride home, chica? I'm not feeling very well. Sorry to disappear on you…" I asked her.

"Sure," she replied. "Got a headache?" Her perceptive eyes glanced over me, noting the paint smeared on my body, the tears in my eyes. When she got upstairs, she would doubtless notice the light cream color of the floor, the walls that were no more painted than when she left. She, of course, wouldn't say anything.

"Something like that," I replied. She turned and walked down the stairs. I followed a few steps behind.

SLEEPING WITH HIS BEST FRIEND

We lingered much too long
across the rumpled bed.
I should have sent him home;
smiled, a gentle hostess,
and closed the door behind you both.

How was I to know
(how could I not)
that when you said good night
you meant goodbye?

And if I should have known
would I have touched that carven face
those pouting lips?

I shut the door behind you alone
and turned to see him smiling there,
knowing why I'd let him stay;
knowing what I would not say
until it was too late.

At times when minds are silent
lips and tongues and thighs can shout
a rough-voiced yes into the sweaty chest
and crumpled sheets.

When he dared me
to tell the truth,
should I have lied?

BLIND

I wake to darkness.

The champagne lingers in my body, and I do not know how long I have been asleep. Perhaps I dozed off briefly during the birthday celebration—I am not used to so much champagne. Maybe I have been asleep for hours, and Joshua has ushered out the guests and turned out the lights.

There is a heaviness across my eyes, something pressing against the skin. I try to bring my hand to my face, to test what feels like silk, or chiffon... and discover my hands are bound behind me. Gently, comfortably, but without any extra give at all. I am curled on my side, my arms behind me, my legs tucked under, blind.

This is probably one of his little games, but I hear no voices, feel no touch of callused hand or stubbled chin. I breathe deeply and open my mouth to scream for him... and a finger lands softly on it, as a feather might, and a stranger's voice whispers, "hush."

I do not know who is here. I do not know who is here with me, in my blue-painted room, in my flannel-sheeted bed. I do not know whether to scream or smile or wait. Maybe I am dreaming.

A hand slips between my legs, parting them gently. This hand is soft, testing, and I am dry as desert, and I do not know if that is what the stranger wants. Apparently not, for he, she, parts my legs even more, and a wet mouth is suddenly moving on me. The mouth plays me like an old friend, tracing a delicate path from inner thigh to hipbone to circle around my clit and back again. This is not Joshua's touch. This is not a rapist's touch.

I try to remember the tongues of all my lovers. All of them, every one, did this at one time or another. The growing fire between my damp thighs is making it hard to think. I am trembling now, as soft hair brushes my hip and a warm tongue thrusts in and out, followed swiftly by one, two, three fingers. And then I am arching, moaning, begging this stranger, and a tongue is tasting my neck and this, this is Joshua, biting softly and the world is starting to dissolve around me... they stop.

Cold hands grasp my breasts and squeeze, hard, forcing a gasp. They twist my nipples cruelly, and I am helpless against this. Tighter and tighter, and then the fingers are replaced by two mouths, biting softer, then harder, until I am pleading, no, don't, noooo...

I do not say stop. One continues and the other slides behind me, and I cannot tell whom it is. Male, though, his hairless chest pressed hard against my back, his erection hard against me. I can feel the texture of his warm skin against my own shivering.

Fingers gently probe my asshole, and I contract, tense. The mouth on my breast stops its assault suddenly, and it is kissing me, a stranger's kiss on my lips and so it is Joshua behind me, unless there are more than two. Fingers return to squeezing nipples, and gentle lips drop butterfly kisses against my mouth, my cheeks, my chin. Fingers—Joshua's, I hope—are cold and wet between my cheeks, sliding in and out and around, going deeper and deeper each moment.

A cock slides between my thighs, rubbing gently against my clit as his hips move forward to meet mine. The man in front of me, a man I do not know, continues to kiss me as his cock strokes my inner thighs, his mouth gently promising, not asking.

I do not remember when I first started telling Joshua my fantasies. The one about sex with a stranger. The one about two people at once. The one about two men at once, two cocks inside me. The one about pain. The one about being blind.

A cock presses against my asshole, insistent, demanding. It pushes forward, and I cannot tell how long it takes to make its way inside. The stranger alternates breast and breast and mouth and neck, at one moment his teeth and Joshua's on opposite sides of my neck, at another so close they might be kissing. Fingers tease my nipples, my clit, rake fiercely along my back and sides and always the cock in my ass is sliding further and further, until it is lodged inside me and I am almost weeping.

Then the stranger slams into me, his cock in my cunt, his smooth chest crushing my breasts and I am crushed between them, and they are kissing me everywhere. The cocks slide in and out, slowly at first, alternating then synchronous and back again. And the stranger is gripping my head between his hands, his thumbs pressed firmly through the cloth against my shut eyes, and Joshua's leg wraps around us both as he thrusts harder and harder; as my moans get louder and louder and he is whispering words of love and the stranger is silent, his chest against my breasts, rubbing and rubbing. And the world once again begins to dissolve, to slow, to freeze with that particular peculiar stillness, as they slam my body between them, and the two cocks erupt, one after another and I cannot tell which is first and the stranger suddenly tears the blindfold from my eyes.

And I come screaming into the light.

MANGO

Manisha drips it down her pointed chin, careless
As she laughs at my plight. Unable to pick up the phone with
Nails and palms dripping with sweet juices. I let it
Go—he will doubtless call again—let him wonder, and
Oh! I would like to lick her clean.

SUMMER

Shade is the only goodness in the Chicago day as we lie entwined
Under the blazing sun and lake wind as
My lips tease with words and breath, promising
Mystery you desire and I regret
Even friendship and lust cannot cross this
Ravine between us.

(for Alex)

MEMORY'S A TRAITOR

Even the touch of your gentle hands cannot erase
Rusty red nights slammed up against
Old bedsprings noisy with use. Roommates
Teased and complained and classes were forgotten
In the heat of Indian summer.
Christ. It's sometimes hard to hate him.

MORNINGSONG

When you sleep, the lines all smooth out of your face. Worry lines, age lines, even the laugh wrinkles at the corner of your eyes that I see all too rarely, disappear into pale softness. I was pressed against your back, asleep, my chest against your spine, my left arm flung over your waist. I wake hours before you would, if left to yourself.

Oh, but I am too cruel to let you sleep. I slide my hand down until it curls around your penis, soft in the morning sunlight. I wait, breathing softly on your neck, too softly to wake you. Soon, warmth of my hand and gentle pressure combine to begin to make you hard; a slow, delightful stiffening.

Gentle, so gentle this must be. I don't want you to wake until I'm ready.

Now comes the difficult part. I must climb over you without waking you, and find a comfortable place halfway down your body, somehow without falling off the bed. You have edged your way almost to falling off yourself, so this is difficult. I must nudge you over, so slowly, hoping you will not wake or roll over into an impossible position. I am lucky this time, and you make room for me, grumbling in your sleep.

You are still hard. My right hand slips down to cup your balls, hanging cool and loose in the morning. My tongue darts out to taste you, salty-sweet, indescribably you. I would know the taste of you anywhere. You are somehow sweeter than any of my other lovers.

I run my tongue up and down your hard length, flicking gently at the tip, caressingly lovingly at the base. My teeth close softly on your cock, and I wonder if you will wake. But no, you sleep on. Good. My mouth encircles your tip, squeezing gently, and traces of salt liquids linger on my tongue.

I begin to slide up and down, so softly. My right hand slides into yours, above my head, over your heart. Your heartbeat is getting faster. As I lick and suck and nibble, I begin to wonder if it's time to wake you. Now, as I rub my cheek against your cock? Now, as I run teeth along its length? Now, as I suck you so hard, go down so far, that I can feel you against my throat, and I am filled with you.

And as you begin to clench muscles in your sleep and move against my face I decide it is time, and raise my head only long enough to say your name clearly. Then you are awake, and your eyes lock briefly, startled, on mine before I dive back on you, my mouth plunging over your hard heat, over and over until the shock of waking is past and you are building and building towards the finish.

And there is no more need to be gentle, and suddenly you are slamming into me and cumming wildly, and I must swallow and swallow again until you are finished. You reach down then and draw me up towards you, pausing only to kiss me briefly and say my name before sliding down to do the same to me.

We are so beautifully matched; body to body. And my heart is pounding as your mouth encircles my hard length, stroking fiercely from base to tip.

Your mouth on my cock, my heart in your hands.

ATTRACTION

The studded black leather collar was hard to miss against Belinda's pale skin, sharp against the soft curve of her throat. I imagined I could see the racing pulse beneath it, unlikely as that was in dim diner light.

I'd never seen her look so beautiful.

It wasn't a romantic place where the four of us had gathered - just a student hangout with good burgers and mediocre pizza. Mark and I had only dessert, the raspberry soda of the Himbeersaft spilling out onto my fingers. I resisted asking her to lick them clean. We'd ordered Thai earlier, before coming to meet Belinda and this new man, this stranger. Not a stranger to her, of course—not quite. They'd known each other for months over the net, and in some ways Geoffrey knew her better than I, who'd only known her well for a few months, or even Mark, who usually shared his bed with her. Though they'd never met in the flesh before that night, it was clear that Belinda's heart was in her throat, and Geoff's eyes were oddly knowing as he watched her.

A master has to know his slave.

He made me uneasy. Some feminist instinct prickled my skin when she waited for his nod, when she lowered her eyes in shame at some minor disobedience. There was a power in those dark eyes, those over-large hands. And though a part of me wanted to rescue Belinda, who clearly didn't want rescuing, a part of me was perhaps… jealous?

There are times when independence is not desirable.

Mark's arm was warm around me as we sat facing them in the wooden booth, dinner over, nobody quite ready to take those first steps out into the warm night. Belinda perhaps having second thoughts about the slave role she enacted with this man, myself wondering whether he'd think himself capable of mastering me, Mark perhaps wondering if he'd sleep alone that night. I don't know what Geoff was thinking.

Sometimes I wonder if he thought at all.

As we left the restaurant to meet some friends at a party, we slid from those pairings. Belinda's breasts soft against me as I wrapped my arms around her and held her back, letting the men walk forward. "Are you all right? Do you know your safeword?", questions serving to reassure a very real anxiety… and assuage an overwhelming curiosity. She laughed, those huge eyes smiling, and hugged me close. I wish I could remember what she said that made me kiss her then… not sure whether I wanted to let her go… not sure what he would do if I didn't.

The night was very dark, and his eyes disappeared into it.

Later, I turned from laughing with an old lover to see Belinda kneeling on a table, legs spread, arms locked behind her head, sweet breasts out-
thrust. My breath caught, and Geoff turned towards me. Smiling, he asked
if I'd like to kiss her. I answered that *I* didn't need his permission... and
slid across the polished wooden table to kiss her deeply, caressing a breast
and feeling an inaudible moan in that pale, bound throat before releasing
her. The crowded room had stilled, and a mixture of desire and shame rose
in me as I slid back into Mark's ready arms. She still knelt there, softly
smiling. That somehow made it almost all right. But even if she'd been crying, I don't know if I would have stopped.

There is something infinitely desirable in helplessness.

And in power. He continued to tease me, perhaps unknowingly,
though I doubt it. Geoff seemed oddly aware of his surroundings. Maybe
that's a necessary quality in a good top. How can you surrender all thought,
all judgement, if you aren't sure that someone is making trustworthy decisions for you? Though he concentrated his attention on Belinda, the one
he'd come to see, after all, he spared a little time to verbally spar with me.
Through that evening, the bus ride home, the next hour or two as we headed slowly, inexorably to bed.

Sometimes you don't want to make choices.

I don't know whether it was fear or desire that kept me in Mark's arms
that night, as he surrendered his room to them, and we took an almost too-
narrow couch. Later, a moment when, lacking a condom, I mastered em-
barrassment and went to knock on their door. A pause, shadowed rustlings,
then "Come in." She was beautiful, bent naked on one knee before him,
her silk hair falling down to shield a flushed face. He was fully dressed, a
wide-stranded whip in his hand.

He requested a kiss in payment for the condom.

It was... more than nice. He pulled away before I did, and I wonder
now what would have happened if I'd pushed him on it, running my hands
across that well-muscled chest, pressing my hot body against his. Would
he have taken me then and there? With her kneeling and watching us, and
Mark waiting out in the other room? Or would he have laughed and
pushed me away, sending me back to Mark like a small child reaching for
something too dangerous?

Uncertainty can be an aphrodisiac.

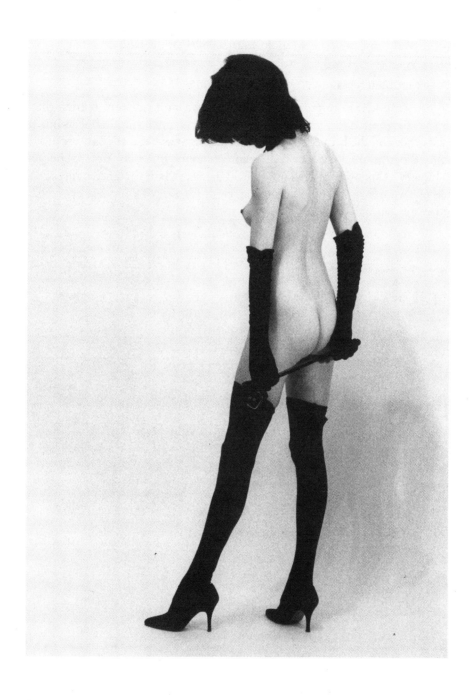

I couldn't let him make that choice, of course, and quickly slipped out the door and back down the darkened hallway. And Mark was waiting, sweet Mark, and the strength in his arms was appealing. We heard her moans and the slap of the whip down the length of the hall, despite closed doors. An effort of will not to run back... to rescue her? to join her?

A muffled scream.

And suddenly I couldn't wait any longer, and we were tearing off clothes far more quickly than I had originally planned, sinking deep into each other and the heat of that first summer night as Belinda's pleasure and pain echoed in the long rooms. I couldn't remember the last time I'd been so hungry... and who can tell how much of it was Mark stretched out golden beneath me, and how much the crack of Geoffrey's whip leaving long red stripes on Belinda's pale skin...

Attraction is composed of desire and danger.

love once rising bright

sleep soft, my heart.

once i might have laid gentle fingers on your thigh, slid
up along the curve of hip while dropping light and
lingering kisses along a sleeping spine. the heavy
dark is warm, and often we have scorned sleep for
endless touchings and midnight burnings—your body
rising bright and shining between my thighs, two beings
blending into one moaning beast. we forget for a
lost moment all the reasons not to love; sweat once
again proclaims that in this, at least, we triumph.

do not fear, my sorrow. though I have no heart for these
essential lies, i will not wake you with reproaches.
sleep soft, and never know what sadness lies in this.

DIANA

"These woods are lovely, dark and deep..." The line kept running through Michael's head as he trudged further up into the Berkshires on that morning, late in September. He shook his head, partly to clear away the mosquitoes that had returned with this brief spate of warm weather, partly in frustration at only being able to remember one line of the poem. He had overdressed, a city boy out in what passed for the wilderness of New England. The sweat dripped down the crease in the center of his forehead to slip under the rim of his wire-frame glasses and collect in small pools on his nose.

This second day of hiking was easier, somehow. Muscles which had been well-toned by college basketball two years ago, had finally started remembering how to move under pressure. Michael hadn't added any flab to his thin frame since leaving college; hours and days spent hunched over a computer had, if anything, only emaciated his long body. A diet of coffee and donuts from the all-night Dunkin' Donuts had kept him going through long nights of programming and debugging. But now - now he had escaped.

Escaped from a city he was growing to hate; New Haven had been bad enough as a student, but it was unbearable outside the guarded precincts of Yale. Escaped from a live-in girlfriend who was becoming more shrewish by the day. Did he even love her anymore? She was still lovely, at least at night. Escaped from her four cats, two dogs, and multitude of small rats in gleaming cages. Michael had escaped for two all-too-brief days of Indian summer sunlight spotting its way through stained glass leaves against a wide and empty sky. And he was determined to make the most of it.

"Two roads diverged in a yellow wood" ...was that even the same poem? Same poet? He couldn't remember. And this wood wasn't yellow. There were still a few green leaves hanging determinedly on the darkening branches, but the overwhelming color was a joyous shouting red across the line of hills. He paused for breath on the trail at a 'lookout point', marked by a small camera signpost. It was stunning, of course. The hill fell away beneath his feet to a deep valley, cleft by a river winding far below. Leaves across the horizon were a patchwork of sunset colors, blazing fiercely in the sunlight. Michael almost felt like breaking out into a Gloria in praise of a God he'd never believed in. He laughed softly to himself as he turned back to the trail.

But there was singing. Somewhere not far ahead, just to the left of the trail, he could hear a woman's voice, high and clear above the murmur of water leading down to the river below. Michael couldn't quite make out the words, so far away, and he began to push his way through the underbrush towards that silver voice.

Sharp thorns scored light tracks along his hands as he pushed them away from his face, and the light dimmed as he went deeper and deeper into the trees. Michael was surprised, and a little disturbed, to know that there was someone else here on this desolate mountain. While he'd known that there were other hikers about, he'd deliberately taken a disused trail, paint faded almost to nothing, to avoid other people. He'd seen nobody for almost two days, and had liked it that way. He'd almost started to miss his girlfriend again.

The brush had been getting harder and harder to push through, but as he persevered he began to hear more voices. He still couldn't make out their words, but low, throaty laughter danced across the still autumn air, pulling him forward through the thick growth. Suddenly, he broke through, almost falling flat onto his face as the trees gave way to a small clearing, a deep pool...and women.

So many women, it seemed at first, a horde of slim legs, shining teeth, tangled hair and soft breasts. For they were naked, all of them, clothes no doubt discarded nearby for the call of that pool, bright with glittering spar-kles, deep as dying. It was a glorious pool, and they matched it. Michael had pulled back instinctively, and he crouched now in the shadow of an old oak, watching avidly. His lips glistened as he licked them over and over. He began counting the women, finding it difficult to concentrate on anything other than the slide of water on smooth, dark skin. None of the seven women were pale; no, tanned golden by weeks of playing in summer sun-light. Their hair was uniformly blond except for one, and she, she was red. Red as the leaves across the hills, red as sunset.

That one was tall, perhaps even taller than Michael. She sat on a rock for a moment listening to the singer standing by the pool, then leaned over to break the song, still unintelligible to Michael, with a kiss deep and long as the pool itself. Then, laughing wildly, she dived down into the water. When she came up, it clung to her body, caressing the line of imperious neck to impossibly high breasts to slender waist and hips and muscled legs, finally dripping off red-painted toes.

Michael didn't know how long he watched before his legs began to cramp. He was sure these women wouldn't appreciate his presence, and so, slowly, regretfully, began to ease his way back from the clearing, into the woods. And then she called him, a low, accented voice sensuous as silk.

"Come out."

Michael stumbled from his hiding place in the shadow of the ancient oak, falling to one knee, hands braced to catch himself. His face and groin were burning as he looked up, though burning for different reasons. She only laughed at him, a rumble of laughter like muted thunder as one of the blond women stepped forward and reached out a hand to help him up. The blond's hand was steady and dry in his damp one, her nails long and sharp and red as blood. She led him over to where the redhead sat on the flat rock, damp with the water dripping down.

She cocked her head, studying him carefully, from the thatch of wind-swept stringy hair, down the length of his sweat-stained clothing, pausing briefly at the all-too-evident bulge in his pants. She didn't look particularly impressed.

"You don't look like a hunter." she said. Michael shook his head, while trying to place her accent. It seemed familiar, somehow, like something he'd heard before, but he couldn't name exactly where.

"I'm just a hiker," he explained, trying his best scapegrace smile, wondering if he'd wandered accidentally onto private property. The paint signs had gotten very faint towards the end of his trail. "I'm just here to admire the….beauty…" and his voice trailed off as his blush deepened.

Michael tried desperately to keep his eyes on her face and off her naked body.

Then she smiled at him, a smile so stunning he was dizzy with the force of it. Her teeth flashed like a model's, bright and sharp in the sunlight. "We like admirers" she said, and with that beckoned to the six blond women, calling them over from their perches on rocks, their games in the water, their rolling in the drying autumn grass and fallen leaves. They came with fragments of red leaf caught in their tangled hair, with clear water drying on golden skin. He had never, never in his life seen women so beautiful.

And then they were touching him. Michael tensed, unsure what to do or say in this totally impossible situation. They murmured gently among themselves, laughing in some foreign language as they eased off his backpack, untied the sweater wrapped around his waist, pulled off his Vikings cap. They began kissing his neck, his chest, his hard nipples as they unbuttoned his cotton shirt and slid it off his shoulders. The blonds ran their uniformly long fingernails down his chest and back as one knelt in front of him, undoing his pants and removing them, dropping sharp kisses on his trembling thighs. Michael lifted his legs, one at a time, blindly.

They took off boots and socks and pants, his gaze still focused on the blurring face of the redhead and her brightly shining eyes. Then, with their hands and mouths moving over him, she leaned over… and kissed him, sliding her tongue deep into his mouth. It was then that he collapsed.

Michael came back to consciousness to find himself erect against the aging oak, the rough bark pressed into the tender skin of back and buttocks. His arms had been drawn carefully back and tied with some sort of cord, maybe vines. She was standing in front of him, smiling that bright smile again. He was still dizzy.

"I have a question for you." she said.

"Well, I have a lot of questions for you!" Michael began to bluster. He was suddenly terrifyingly, exhilaratingly sure that he would not be seeing his girlfriend, his job, their apartment or her rats again. Now that he had been stripped of his clothing, he felt oddly free to gaze his fill, and his eyes drank in the curves and planes of her body, broken only by a patch of flaming hair.

She seemed to enjoy his gaze, continuing to smile as she watched his eyes watching her. Then she spoke again.

"What do you want?" A clear danger was present in her voice, but a promise lay beneath it—an offer of something Michael couldn't quite grasp.

Time seemed to still and thicken so that Michael had all the time he needed to remember: the days of college when he and his friends, self-proclaimed geniuses, would stay up till dawn promising to see the world and taste its women in wide open fields and hot dark rooms; the clarity of nights without sleep as he talked and fucked and laughed with a girl with wide dark eyes who'd left him when once he slept too late; dancing naked in the rain, all alone. But closer was job, cats, safety, overpowering fear, and the love of a woman probably still asleep back home.

And now he knew how much he loved her after all, so much more than either of them had ever thought. She was cool and calm, like a long drink of water to a thirsty man, a quiet presence in his heart. What did he want? He almost answered, 'to go home'. But he'd gotten too much sleep lately, it seemed, and the lady was fire before him.

"You." he answered, suddenly certain, suddenly sure.

And then she was laughing above him as she reached out and sliced apart the bonds with impossibly sharp fingernails. The women surrounded them, touching them everywhere it seemed as her skin slid against his ready body and she bent to kiss his neck. That was the first and only pain, a sudden sharp tearing though he did not scream as he worshipped her with strong limbs and violent burning thrusts.

She rose to meet him, her red hair falling around him in streams of blood and fire, their long red nails raking down his back. And so Michael rose to brief ecstasy, fully conscious, fully clear that nothing, nothing could be beyond this.

Hours later, they had long since bathed the last traces of blood away, and they were once again beautiful in the moonlight. The wildness had faded for a while, sated by that long orgy in the sunset splendor of fallen leaves. The blond women were dancing slowly and languorously in the outpouring of the full moon. On Diana's face for a moment was something that on another might be mistaken for regret; but it passed quickly. He had been lost from that first moment, after all. And then she joined them in their dance, and it grew wild once again.

Note: Some may claim that Diana should have been virgin; but I don't have much faith in the virtues of virginity.

DIALOGUE

The couple lies intertwined. His left hand rests casually on a small right breast; her hands are pressed against a slightly hairy chest. Dim light falls on them through a white-curtained window above the queen-size bed, creating odd shadows in the curve of young bodies.

HE: "What are you thinking?"

SHE: "Nothing much. Why?"

HE: "You have a funny look on your face."

SHE: "I was just thinking how much I like this."

HE: "Like what, exactly?"

SHE: "How much I like the feel of your rough hair against the palms of my hands. And my thigh between your legs. And …"

HE: "And?"

SHE: "And your cock pressing against my stomach."

HE: "You like that?"

SHE: "Yes."

HE: "Good. What else do you like? What do you want me to do to you?"

She hesitates.

HE: "C'mon… tell me."

SHE: "I'd really like it if…"

HE: "Yes?"

SHE: "If you started to play with my breast. Not just the nipple … if you took my whole breast in your hand, and squeezed it, and rubbed it. After you do that for a while, it gets so sensitive … then when you touch the nipple, it's like there's a current running right through me."

HE: "And after that?"

SHE: "After that… I'd like you to lower your mouth to it. And take the nipple between your teeth, gently. Play with it. Bite it a little—not too hard. I don't like it really hard until I'm very aroused. After a while, switch to the other nipple. Alternate between them, and run your tongue and teeth in the hollow between my breasts, and along the side and back of my neck, sucking as you go."

HE: "And my hands? What should they be doing?"

SHE: "Run your hands along my sides, and once I'm shivering from what you're doing, rake your nails down my back. Cup my buttocks in your broad palms, and squeeze them. Pull me close to you, so that your cock is pressed hard against me. Perhaps you could slide it between my legs, for a while, so that it's pressed against my clit. When you rock back and forth like that, it's almost as good as when you're inside me."

HE: "Do you want my fingers in you, rubbing in and out? Two fingers, three? Should we try the whole hand this time? Or would you rather have my mouth on your clit, my tongue tracing circles around it, then sucking it, soft, then hard, running my teeth along it …?"

SHE: "Not this time, I think. I'm too hungry for your cock inside me. When I'm trembling and moaning, roll onto your back and lift me up until you can impale me on your cock. I'll slide down very very slowly, with your hands on my hips, guiding me. Finally I'll come to rest against you, and then…"

HE: "Yes?"

SHE: "Then, I'd like you to stay very very still. Let me move on you, rubbing back and forth so gently at first … not lifting at all, barely moving."

HE: "You're killing me …"

SHE: "Hush. After a little while, I'd go faster, but with that same movement, your cock deep inside me and my clit rubbing against you in that way it only does when I'm riding you. When I start to moan again, I'd like you to take my breasts in my hands again, and play with them like you did before. But don't move otherwise, please. Hold yourself rigid underneath me till I come, and collapse on top of you."

HE: "Then can I move? Please?"

She laughs.

SHE: "Yes, then you can move. Let me breathe for a moment, then roll us over, so I can feel all of your weight on top of me. Then fuck me, slow at first, then hard and fast, or however you'd like to. Someday, I'll like to be fucked till I faint."

HE: "I'll keep that in mind."

SHE: "I hope…"

HE: "What?"

SHE: "I hope this is what you wanted—I hope I answered your question. I couldn't say any of this out loud, you know. I hope writing it is good enough…"

INTERVIEW WITH A PANEL OF INTERNET EROTICA WRITERS

The Writers

Real Name: Mary Anne Mohanraj (your host for this interview)
E-mail: maryanne@iam.com
Web: http://www.iam.com/maryanne/
Type of erotica: generally realistic, often queer, soft and hard-core. Her stories are available on her Web page, through occasional reposts, and in the rec.arts.erotica archives.
Published in a variety of magazines, including Puritan.
Also writes science fiction, fantasy, horror, poetry and mainstream lit.

Pseudonym: The Flying Pen (FP)
E-mail: an5977@anon.penet.fi
Type of erotica: "hard-core, fantasy, straight, lesbian, fetish-specific…every story is different. I try to make the sex scenes describe the sensory aspects of the experience in detail, sometimes graphically, sometimes not."
His stories are available on alt.sex.stories.
Recently published a fetish story in a small private fetish magazine.
Also writes science fiction and fantasy.

Pseudonym: Jordan Shelbourne (JS)
E-mail: jordan@u36.kwnet.on.ca
Type of erotica: "Most of the stuff I've put out so far has been straight, and I'd probably call it hard-core—I mean, I describe all the body parts. I have other stuff in the works—fantasy, for instance, and some soft-core stuff, and some things that are a bit more fetishistic. Most of my stuff is straight but open-minded: it's implicit and sometimes explicit that the characters are involved in a lot of different scenes besides what's directly shown in the story.
His stories are available on alt.sex.stories and rec.arts.erotica, and other people's Web pages.
Publishes textbooks, magazine articles and sketch comedy shows under his real name.
Also writes science fiction, fantasy, mystery, thrillers, humor and mainstream fiction.

Real name: Yosha Bourgea (YB)
Pseudonym: Grendel.
E-mail: grendel@camelot.bradley.edu
Web: http://rhf.bradley.edu/~grendel/
Type of erotica: I don't know that it's possible to define it by type; I write what interests me, and that is constantly in flux. I'd say my stuff is pretty consistently straight, not sf, and rarely concerned with measurements, bells 'n' whistles, or frou-frou.
His stories are reposted periodically to alt.sex.stories, are also available in the rec.arts.erotica archives, on his home page, and someone in Israel translated his story "Aphatos" into Hebrew.

Published in Cyanosis Magazine, Broadside (of Bradley University), local zines and several newspapers.
Also writes horror, magic realism, potboilers with twist endings, and unclassifiable realistic stuff. Also poetry and screenplays.

Real name: Christine Faltz (CF)
E mail: cmfaltz@panix.com
Type of erotica: Soft-medium, all genders, no incest/bestiality/coprophilia. Lots of Star Trek erotica.
Not yet published in print.
Also writes fiction, poetry, science fiction, fantasy.

[MM] We've gathered together some of the top writers of erotica on the Internet, writers who are known worldwide for the quality of their writing and the popularity of their stories, to ask them some questions about their field—what it's like, where it's at, and where it's going. The first question I asked them is probably the question I get asked most often as an erotica writer—why do I do it? Why do they choose to write erotica, despite the social stigmas attached to it?

[Yosha Bourgea] For personal stimulation—but I guess that applies to any kind of writing, doesn't it? Because it's still dangerous. Because it's often done very poorly, and I like the "challenge" of doing it well. Because I find sex interesting as a concept.

[Christine Faltz] I write erotica because people like to read it and I like to write it, and because I like the controversial nature of doing so.

[YB] Yeah, don't forget the pleasure of pleasure. It's exciting to write and exciting to read. Probably no other genre produces such an immediate, visceral response, with the exception of horror. Now, you can make a joke of that (as you can with horror) but the thought of using my skill with words to provoke emotional or physical arousal in others quite frankly turns me on—and I mean that as an artist as well as a sexual human being.

[Jordan Shelbourne] Why do I write anything? Because the story shows up in my head. I was rewriting stories off the net, just to learn, and I was really pleased about something I'd written when I suddenly realized what a shit I'd feel like if someone did that to one of my stories. So I threw out the other person's story, substituted elements from my own life, and made other stuff up.

Actually, we're answering two questions here, how we got started and why we continue. Since I write under a pseudonym—a nom de net, as it were—I'm not being as brave as the others in writing in the face of censure. I continue because I want to. My friends know I write erotica. Maybe someday, I'll have to choose between writing erotica and writing other fiction.

[Flying Pen] I write erotica because it's fun. I originally got into doing it because I didn't like the quality of most of the stories on a.s.s. Instead of complaining, I decided to prove that I could do better. And my first story got such an overwhelming, positive response that I kept doing it.

[YB] Same here. I guess some people are satisfied with endless combinations of four-letter words, but I found most of the erotica out there as stimulating as paste. Why can't people be subtle and explicit at the same time? I told myself I was going to write a *real* erotic story, one that had a story, with real people, not just cardboard cutouts. So I did.

[MM] Yes, that's how I started too; reading stories on rec.arts.erotica and thinking, 'I can do better than this.' I also found that I got a huge, positive response when I first posted stories to the net, which certainly encouraged me to keep writing them. What sort of response have you gotten?

[CF] Very positive, very few "freaks", rarely propositioned by my fans. I receive a lot of fan mail with suggestions, praise, and requests.

[YB] So far, the responses have been almost completely positive. One person told me not to quit my day job, but other than that, most people have told me my erotica is head, shoulders and genitals above most of the crap out there. That's good to hear.

[FP] Positive. Some have actually asked me about characters, and debated with me on certain points of the story, not just the sex. My wife gets very aroused when reading some of the sex scenes, but she enjoys the stories and the characters.

[MM] I find it fascinating (and at times very touching) how so many readers are willing and eager to tell me how my stories have touched their lives—and occasionally tell me all about their lives. Generally, I enjoy such personal details, but I have had a few readers send me irritating propositions and obnoxious mail. Do any of you have any horror stories to share?

[JS] Not in the sense you mean. I did have one fellow send me e-mail every six pages as he read the story, letting me know how he was enjoying it…right up to the ending, which he said was "cheesy" but he never bothered to explain why. For me, that was a horror story. :-)

[FP] Just one. I wrote a story about an interracial relationship. I got flamed by a few assholes, but the public (newsgroup) and private support I got overwhelmed it, and I actually wound up talking to a few foreign students who were ignorant of the black experience, and whose reactions to black people was uniformly fear. I think I did some good.

[YB] Several men have tried to pick up on me over e-mail, mostly because my name sounds feminine to those unfamiliar with Russian literature and I don't make a point of announcing my gender or sexual preference unless it's relevant to the topic of conversation. Once they find out that I'm a straight male, most of my beaux vanish without a trace, but one fella got very upset, accusing me of being a cock-teasing faggot. I posted his letters on a.s.s. and told him to piss off. He did.

[MM] We hear a lot about women on the Internet—how few of us there are; how harassed we can be in such a male environment. Surprisingly, I know I've only received a few obnoxious pieces of e-mail out of the thousands of letters from my readers, and the one fan who actually called me was both apologetic and surprised that he'd actually reached me. I'd like to ask Christine whether she feels especially harassed because she writes erotica?

[CF] No, not at all.

[MM] How about the men? Do you get hard-line feminists giving you a hard time for writing erotica? Have you ever been accused of exploiting women?

[YB] Not so far, but most of my erotica is miles from exploitative—it tends toward the sensual, subtle and sensitive. I keep most of my hard-core stuff to myself, both because it's not very good and because it's personal in nature.

[JS] No, but I was once told that, though my story was fine, all erotica needs a "woman's touch." She wouldn't explain that, either. I have terrible luck with getting explanations from people. (laugh)

[YB] Well, I think Virginia Woolf was right when she said that to write well, one cannot be exclusively a man or a woman; one must be man womanly or woman-manly. Failure to do this usually shows up in flat, unbelievable people. And that (IMHO) makes for flat, unremarkable erotica. But I don't think women have a monopoly or anything like it on eroticism or understanding what makes sex sexy.

[FP] I find that I get a lot of positive feedback from female readers (and male readers who appreciate what my story did for their SO) . But then most people who are going to be offended by the "exploitation and degradation inherent in a male-female sexual act" usually don't bother reading alt.sex.stories. For the most part, the women in my stories are living, breathing, thinking beings; it's very rare that I reduce a woman to being a bunch of sex parts that are readily available for _use_ by another person. If I do, there's always a plot-based reason for it.

[JS] I agree whole-heartedly with the Pen. I think all the characters should be believable. I try to make them all real.

[MM] So your women are living beings? Are they women from your own life? That's probably the second-most popular question I get, especially about the more kinky stories—where do you get your ideas?

[YB] Any writer who gives a single, definable answer to that question is either a liar or a plagiarist. For me, it's bits of everything. Oddly enough, the bits that are based in reality are usually mistaken for pure fiction, and vice versa. But the bottom line is that I'm a thief. I'll use whatever I think I can get away with.

[FP] Tough one. I've written one true story among the six or seven I've written. People and places are liberally taken from my world; and all of the women are based on women I have met, or seen. Their characters may be extrapolated musings with no bearing on reality, but I just can't write a sex scene with a complete figment of my imagination.

[MM] So are the stories based on your own lives, or your friends lives' or chunks of imagination?

[JS] All of the above. The bathroom incident in Unwrap Party happened to me. For some years, I was a magnet for the sexually dysfunctional—most of the women I dated had been raped or abused or somehow made to feel sexually inadequate. Their lives have given me more than enough material, if I want to use it. At least in fiction, I can give them happy endings. Some stuff is just imaginary. A lot of elements that go into my stories come out of casual fantasies of mine. I think, "Gosh, she's cute (or sometimes, he's attractive), but we're just such opposites. What would it take to get her (or him) into bed?"

Actually, no one asks me where I get my ideas (I guess my stuff is just too vanilla). I get asked mostly, "Are you going to write any more about those characters?" and second, "Have you *done* all of the stuff you write about?"

Without a feel of reality in a story, I keep thinking, "This writer doesn't know what he's talking about." Realism doesn't mean the story has to be realistic—I read vampire stories, for instance—but the details have to convince me. They have to either remind you of how something similar was for you, or convince you that, yeah, if you were a nineteen-year-old virgin, that's how it would feel. This feeling of reality does two things for the story—first, it separates it from all of those fourth-generation copies of stories that are as expendable as tissue, and second, it sets the reader up to believe the *really* impossible stuff.

[YB] Sure. Real-life reality mostly abides by social mores, so a lot of the stuff that erotica writers explore doesn't happen. On the other hand, pure fantasy that has no relation to real life isn't dangerous, and therefore not very stimulating. It's when you can make the story seem as real as possible, and then introduce something desirable but unlikely into the midst of that reality, that the erotic becomes really erotic. For me, anyways.

[MM] Which rather begs the question of what you as authors find erotic, and what are your favorite subjects to write about?

[YB] The unspoken, the forbidden, the taboo. I work from pictures I see in my mind, rather than events or plots.

[CF] I like erotica with a plot, real people and real scenarios. If I can I like to preach about something in my stories; I try to be subtle but it doesn't always work.

[FP] Current fantasies; they provide an instant gratification the first couple of times. Taking a past situation in my life and playing "what if I had…" Alternately, taking an idea and twisting it some. _Night Music_ (by response, my most popular work,) was a vampire story with sex in it. My favorite story (it almost wrote itself) was an idea from the universe of another net.author, and I took his settings and turned it into a pretty neat (and pretty hot, judging by my wife's reaction) story.

[JS] I like to write about people who don't think they fit in anymore, because I was a loner for a lot of years. I also like the idea of teaching and exploring options together. _Pushing the Envelope_ was conceived as a storyline that would let me do just about anything in terms of sexual variation.

I don't know about anyone else, but I look for erotica by women searching in part for that kind of insight.

[MM] I've enjoyed writing about the Internet, and I have to wonder, how has the existence of the Internet impacted your writing? We certainly hear a lot nowadays about the power of the net, and I've found newsgroups like a.s.s. and r.a.e. very useful—they've provided a great forum for my stories. What influence has the net had on your stories?

[CF] All I can say about the net is that it has allowed me to have a great deal of fun, has given me a fantastic forum (worldwide) to get reactions to my writing, and has allowed me the relative anonymity of the medium.

[FP] I enjoy the feedback, and the ego-gratification. To know that I *can* do it, and do it well helps keep me going. Some people have offered useful critiques (I tend to write long stories, and I am not beyond taking suggestions) that have been incorporated into current and future efforts.

Also, I don't think I would be writing if it hadn't been for the net; a.s.s. is a fairly easy forum; it's difficult to get booed off of that particular stage, and there's a lot of confidence in knowing that at the least, you'll get pretty much silence.

[JS] They say that every writer needs a "throwing book"—something he or she can throw against the wall, crying, "I can write better than this crap!" That's what the net has been for me. Despite the fact that some very talented writers put their work on the net, there's a lot of crap. Well, I started to write erotica because of that crap. Plus, it's easy to put your stuff on-line, so you don't have to worry about the crushing rejection when an editor returns your story. There are no editors!

So the net has offered me a no-risk place to publish. Since I work at a company with access, it doesn't cost me anything.

[YB] It has given me a much larger audience than I would have had otherwise, as well as a much more accepting community than I would have been able to find in Real Life. My first notable erotica, "Aphatos," was written on my computer in a few heated hours (highly unusual for me) and posted on a.s.s. shortly thereafter.

[MM] The net certainly offers some interesting publishing opportunities—I met the editor of Puritan when he came across my Web page and read some of my stories. Writers have also been hearing a lot about the exciting possibilities of 'hypertext fiction', an umbrella term that covers many different types of writing, including multi-person stories written by people on other sides of the world, Web stories in which the reader can click on different words to take them to different parts of the story, and much more. What do you see as the future of on-line writing?

[YB] This is an area of study that interests me a great deal. I've done some research, and I think on-line writing is going to explode. At the moment, copyright status of on-line writing is shaky, but it will probably be stable within a year. The big problem for many aspiring authors is reaching an audience. It's difficult to get published these days, regardless of talent. The great advantages of the net are speed and availability; for not much money, I can send what I've written to thousands and thousands of people across the world. That excites me as a writer, as a journalist, and as a political activist. I know the net suffers from hyperbole, but my personal experience leads me to believe there really _is_ something revolutionary about the possibilities of on-line communication.

[FP] Hypertext fiction, and interactive stories have great potential, but someone is going to have to go nearly broke trying to get it to the public consciousness.

[JS] I've yet to see any hypertext fiction that really works. Linear fiction is difficult to do well, and I can only imagine that hypertext fiction is exponentially more difficult.

The net is self-publishing on a vast scale. The distribution area of your work is incredible, and totally unreliable. It will probably go worldwide— unless it doesn't. Every article or Web page is a home-made newsletter, and the net is this giant mimeograph machine that's spewing copies of everyone's home newsletter to everyone else.

When you look at the Web and Usenet, it just proves that 90% of everything is crud. There will always be great writers and good writers and mediocre writers who are getting better, and there will always be a lot of crud. I'd rather read the former than the latter. In traditional publishing, editors weed out a lot of the crud. I think you'll see a lot more moderated newsgroups, mailing lists, special access Web pages that provide the good 10% for their audience.

[CF] Because I am visually impaired it would be fantastic if everything printed were available to me online. As for erotica on the net, it is seriously endangered at the moment. Net erotica is in crisis; the US government appears to think it has the right to suspend the First Amendment with respect to cyberporn. As a new mother I don't know how much time I'll have for combatting this travesty but you can be sure I'll be fighting.

[MM] The presence of sexual materials on the net is certainly causing an uproar among certain political groups—what do all of you think about the proliferation and popularity of sex-oriented areas on-line, such as x-rated chat rooms, porn magazines, nude photo sites and phone sex ads?

[JS] Hey—sex sells. You're not going to get an argument from *me* that people aren't interested in sex. They certainly are. And sex services move quickly into new frontiers, whether it's the old West or Internet. I sometimes wonder why the pictures are so popular. On the other hand, (1) they're "free" and (2) the pictures are always changing (that's the so-called Coolidge effect) and (3) on-line sex can sidestep local morality. I saw pictures on Usenet showing penetration, bondage, anal sex, and bestiality long before they were legal in my home town—some of those pictures I still can't buy.

[FP] Sex on the Internet is a problem with a fundamental American (my bias) dichotomy: we sell it, we want it, but we don't want to admit it exists. It is this which makes sex on the Internet so popular; it's the feeling of "getting away with something" you couldn't do (for whatever reasons) in person. If there was no demand for it, it wouldn't sell (phone sex, cyber sex services). Sex-focused Web pages are a matter of those people who acknowledge that fundamental drive, and don't really have much to fear from those who would try to hide it.

[YB] Human nature. Happens in every medium. People are fascinated by the forbidden, which is the only reason most smut ever gets produced or consumed. The great majority of sexually oriented material on-line isn't worth the bandwidth it takes up, but it's harmless. The best defense (and the only effective defense) against bad taste is good taste; censorship is a waste of everyone's time. Finally, to the good stuff out there—the Sen. Jim Exon Memorial webpage, Reclaiming the Erotic, etc.—I just say YES. Sex is good. Let's have more.

[MM] You certainly won't get any argument from us about that! It seems to me that there are great possibilities for sex on-line, in all its new and exciting forms, and I certainly think that all of you are doing a great deal in both elevating the quality of what's available and hopefully in legitimizing on-line erotica. Do you have any final comments before we wind this up?

[FP] Yeah. Censorship. The idea that "We think 'x' is bad, therefore it shouldn't exist" really stinks. It exists in real life, and the net is a slightly distorted mirror of real life. Slightly distorted because the anonymous nature of the net allows people to virtually do and say things they wouldn't in real life. I agree that something has to be done; there are locking mechanisms available for Web pages and access controls to newsgroups. Lastly, there is the issue of parental control; it's not a playground to leave your kids unsupervised in. If you don't want your children exposed to the myriad of people and thoughts and ways of life out in the world, then don't let them on the net without supervision. You would not drop a kid off in downtown New York with an unlimited supply of cash and say "I'll be back to pick you up in a few hours." .... But making the net a computerized Disney channel is not the answer. There are too many things we can learn from the other people on the net.

[YB] Sex is woefully misunderstood in this and many other cultures. At root, it's as prosaic as eating and shitting, not this great pink mystical bauble of a Santa Claus we've all been fed. That said, it also offers fantastic opportunities for art and beauty (childbirth being a prime example). It can be both—a simple fact of life AND a powerful experience—but only if we cut out this taboo bullshit. Children are never too young to learn about sex and eroticism. Every instance in which sex and tragedy have combined results from people not being honest and open about sex. Honest sex never hurt anyone. I guess the point of this rant is that whatever can be done to help people understand sex, eroticism, and their own relationship to it is good and worthwhile in my book.

[MM] Mine too, certainly, and I hope this article has contributed to that understanding. Well, I hope you've all enjoyed this interview, and I'd like to take a moment to thank these authors who so kindly agreed to be interviewed: Jordan Shelbourne, Christine Faltz, Yosha Bourgea, and the Flying Pen. I encourage all readers with net access to take a little time to look up their work on-line—it's writers like these who are keeping erotica alive and healthy, and readers like you who keep them going!

REUNION

His shiny black shoes almost glowed in the dingy room. She kept her eyes fixed on them as he ordered their breakfast. Eggs the way she liked them, sunny-side up, like open eyes. Toast on the side, no jam. Just tea for him. He'd complain about the tea, of course. Why couldn't they boil the water? How long had they left the tea, already steeped, sitting in the dirty glass pot?

She switched her gaze from shoes to plate. Forcing herself to eat slowly. He rattled the way he always did when he was nervous. Clattered the mug down and spilled tea over the sides, which the waitress wiped up easily on the red-and-white checkered vinyl tablecloth. They were there for what seemed like hours before he took her arm and pulled her out the door.

The motel was only across the street. Instead, he cut through the fields and she followed. Fields of golden sunflowers, scattered patches of Queen Anne's lace and bright purple tufted things. Scratchy fields. When she pulled off her dress and lay down on it, she could still feel the stubbly grass and stubborn stones beneath her. Every breeze brought thousands of tiny grasses brushing against her bare body, each stem feeling like skittering insects. She clenched her fingers into the damp soil to hold her there, so she wouldn't leap up and run naked onto the highway.

When he came, much later, he was crying. Maybe she was too. It was hard to tell with the sun beating down and sweat still dripping down her face and onto his beaky nose. She hushed him with soft kisses. His legs wrapped convulsively around hers, broken promises falling out of his mouth like rain, or tears, or children. Running off into the grass.

Slowly their pulses calmed. They slept under a cloak of her mustard hair, her head nestled under his sharp chin.

***

Maybe it would be like that. But more likely it wouldn't. Janie stepped away from the phone once more, to sit in a shrinking pool of sunlight by the window. The calico cat leapt momentarily from the mantel into her lap, long enough to leave a jagged gash along her thigh. Janie's fingers clenched tightly in the space the cat had been. Too late.

LADY

She was trying very hard not to look scared. Scared was dangerous. Scared had gotten her married, gotten her beaten, gotten her raped in her home and on the road. If she'd learned one thing in the last three weeks it was this: sexy was a whole lot more useful than scared.

***

It was a short run from La Porte to Champaign, but it was the last run of a long day of contract hauling. Mike was tired and wanted to get some sleep, so he almost didn't stop for the slim figure in white, holding out a pitiful thumb. The glare of headlights was unforgiving, picking out every detail of tired skin and soiled clothing. But there was still something desirable about those curves, and it wouldn't be human to expect a lonely man to turn down a shot at them. He pulled over.

"Where ya going?" she called up, hand over her face to shield against the glare.

"Champaign."

"Is that anywhere near Chicago?"

Mike shook his head, bewildered. "Lady, where are you coming from?"

"Connecticut. But I lost my map, and my last ride wasn't going any closer than this. This is the best I could do." She sounded stubborn. Like she was gonna get to Chicago if she had to go through Austin, San Jose, and St. Paul to do it.

"Well, I'm not going to Chicago, but you're not likely to get another ride tonight. Why don't you come to Champaign with me and maybe we can find you someplace to sleep?" Mike smiled at her, the smile that had won over a hundred waitresses from La Porte to Tallahassee.

She didn't hesitate a minute. As he pushed open the passenger door, she swung a small hand up to the handle and hauled her body inside, landing with a muffled thump on the padded seats. He'd gotten them covered in fake fur a couple of years ago. They were starting to wear through, but they were still a whole lot kinder to bare skin than the original vinyl.

She had nothing with her. No purse, no backpack. Mike had picked up a lot of hitchhikers in his time, and every single one of them, no matter how down and out she looked, had something to carry that last photo, that small hoard of cash. Judging by the tightness of her jeans, this lady wasn't hiding much of anything in them either.

She swung the door closed, and settled back with a deep sigh. Mike glanced over at her. In the gentle moonlight she looked a whole lot better. Soft curves were outlined under a thin lace top, curves shielded only by a fall of pale wheat hair. Not quite your typical blue-eyed blond, though. Her eyes were ice blue, her skin ghost-pale. She looked like she'd blow away in the lightest breeze, or melt in a summer storm.

"What's your name, lady?"

She stiffened. "I'd rather not tell you. Do you need a name?" The lady suddenly looked almost dangerous. Cornered. Terrified.

"Nah, that's okay. Although you could have made something up and I would've believed you. How 'bout I just call you 'lady'?"

She laughed softly, relaxing again. "That's fine." Mike glanced over to catch that smile, and suddenly realized that she wasn't really relaxed. Her hands were clenched into tight balls, her fingers digging into sweaty palms. She lifted her head, watching him watching her. She smiled. Mike's breath caught at the sexiness in that smile. Suddenly he didn't want to start the truck again. He wanted nothing more than to peel off those tight jeans, and shred that lace top.

He wanted to dig his fingers into those soft breasts, to squeeze the hard nipples he could see stretching the fabric. Funny how after so many women the curve of a full breast could still drive him crazy. If he didn't start moving soon, he'd take her right now. Mike preferred his women willing, though, and this one still looked scared. Maybe in a couple of hours she'd be a little more willing. Maybe in a couple of hours, he wouldn't be quite so patient.

Mike took a deep breath and started the truck again, heading back onto the highway, going west. She was silent beside him for a long time, maybe an hour or so till they hit I-57 and started heading south. The moon hid behind a cloud and the only light was from Indiana stars. Then suddenly she started talking, opening her mouth and letting the words pour out.

The lady told him why she ran, the man behind the story. Mike listened to her dry-eyed, making the appropriate noises. It was a story to break a heart, if you'd never heard one like it before. Unfortunately, too many of the waitresses told the same tale.

She was beautiful in pain, thin and drawn taut under the tension. As they pulled into a deserted rest stop, half an hour from Champaign, she had just finished telling him about her journey. The truckers who'd offered her a ride in exchange for a bed. The ride before last had taken her bag, her money, her clothes.

She might have died that night if a hooker hadn't taken pity on her and given her something to wear. Naked women didn't last long on the streets. The flood of words dried to a trickle, then a halt, in pace with the motion of the truck.

"You're beautiful." he told her. It was a line that had worked many times before, perhaps because he meant it every time. All Mike wanted was to treat her gently, to kiss away those lines on her forehead. He wanted to taste the salt at the back of her neck, to give her pleasure she had never known. Mike wanted to run his hands down her long limbs, to tilt the soft seat back as far as it would go, and go down on her until she screamed. To treat the lady better than some of the bastards on the road would.

The line worked this time too, it seemed. Her body softened, lips tilting up to smile at him, to beg for a kiss. She closed her eyes then. Mike leaned across to her—only then did he notice the hands still clenched, fingernails digging bruised crescents into her palms. At that moment, he knew what else she'd gotten from the hooker; she'd learned how to convince the johns that she was enjoying what they did to her. And, being such a lady, she'd learned to do it with grace. Mike pulled away abruptly, painfully.

"I gotta go. There's a ladies' room in back." Mike said, as he swung down out of the cab.

When he came back, she was still sitting there, looking slightly stunned, slightly scared.

"Hey, listen—" he said as he gunned the engine, "I gotta friend who lives in Champaign; runs a trinket shop in the plaza there. She's a little crazy, and doesn't answer to her real name anymore, but she's a good kid. Why don't you stay with her tonight? You oughta be able to find someone going up to Chicago in the morning."

"That... sounds good," the lady replied hesitantly.

"Do you have somebody to stay with up there?" Mike asked.

She still looked surprised, and her eyes were dead, but there was a bit of a smile in her voice as she said, "Yes, actually. A girlfriend from high school, working on the South Side now."

"Good," Michael said. He started whistling then, some tune he didn't remember the words to. She didn't say anything and he didn't stop whistling until they pulled into the driveway of a large house at 4 am. He left her there at the door, his friend small and sleepy-eyed beside the lady.

YOU'LL UNDERSTAND WHEN YOU'RE OLDER, DEAR

Have you ever been in love?
Really in love?
I mean the fairy-tale kind,
with blue skies and never lies,
perfect skin and angel eyes,
and the only argument
is over who loves whom
more?

Me neither.

Have you ever been fucked?
Really fucked?
Bang your head against the
metal bedpost—never notice,
soft sheets or concrete—
makes no difference,
screaming something and if
it's the wrong name who
fucking gives a damn
god yes,
fucked?

Yeah.

Some days, you take what you can get.
Some day, maybe you'll be glad of it.

FEATHER

There was an angel on my bed. Really. An incandescent, feathery white-winged, ten-foot-tall angel. Don't ask how it got there. I don't even go to Mass. In any case, no nun I ever talked to mentioned the possibility of multiply-gendered, stark naked, holy visitations. Not even the saints got naked angels.

What did I do? What would any sane person do in that situation? The cat fled, squealing as if all the legions of hell were after it. Perhaps the Inquisitors had been right about black cats. I shut the bedroom door, leaned against it, and waited. Then it beckoned.

It was definitely an it. When it wasn't definitely a he, or a she. Have you ever, on a melting August afternoon, ignored your mom's yells to close the fridge door and just stood there, basking in the tingle? The angel, it glowed. Only it glowed heat so hot it froze you—or maybe it was cold so cold it burned.

I stepped over to the bed. The sheets weren't on fire or covered in ice. Just me. The angel never said a word, although later I would have sworn it was singing hallelujahs the whole time. My roommate never heard a thing. The angel drew me down to her breasts, the long white feathers dissolving into rose-pink skin. No pores.

Later, when my clothes had disappeared with a brush of angel wings (they never did come back), I brushed my nipples against hers, only to find the feathers had come back. It wasn't until I sat, impaled, that I noticed he had pointed teeth.

My roommate didn't even hear my screams, as I rode the angel's hard body, locked in an embrace of biting teeth and engulfing wings. I don't know what angel semen does to human flesh—the angel shifted right after my orgasm, gone out of me as if it had never been there at all. The breasts reappeared and disappeared at will. The wings never changed, though.

Tired, I struggled not to fall asleep, and it grinned its first grin as I watched it slowly dissolve into a tacky plastic crucifix on a blue-bead rosary. Then the rosary dissolved too.

You figure out why it came. Maybe it fell in love, or it's a new kind of ad campaign, or I'm going crazy, or Lucifer's gonna approach me with a real sweet deal and all the angel slaves I want thrown into the bargain. Me, I have to go to work in the morning, and if it weren't for the feather-shaped burn mark on my chest, I'd put it all down to a momentary psychotic episode and try not to stress too much. As is, I'm just waiting for the men in white coats or some clearer instructions.

If there's a God watching over me, wanting something from me, then It's going to have to be a lot more convincing to talk me into joining Its side. But if you see Sister Agnes anytime soon, tell her for me....nah, don't tell her anything. I don't think her universe could hold an angel like that one. I do have a bit more hope for a God who'd create a universe that does. Maybe that's all It wanted.

DREAMS OF A LOVER

she leaned back in the wooden chair against institution
green walls of the college library, staring out through glass
doors into the thundering night, and my struggling.

wrestling the door open I dripped my way inside, only to be
told 'sorry, we're closed, we just hadn't locked up yet' from
one of the night guards sitting next to her smiling.

but she rescued me, with a promise that she would lock up
when she left and an explanation for me. she an english
graduate student who worked at the library on saturday nights.

shivering she saw me, and made me take off sodden sneakers
and sweatshirt in an empty corner, draped over rickety
chairs, careful not to damage books that were both our hearts.

she wore grey skirt and white poet's shirt, though she wrote
no poetry only criticism, with soft chinese slippers in blue-
green to match her eyes and gold dragons.

miraculously we matched sizes and she insisted I wear the
slippers as we walked through the overhanging rows and
she listened silent while I talked of love and literature.

hours later, rain had stopped but she had me keep the slippers
as I went out into a breaking blue-gold dawn to match her eyes
every sharp cobblestone clearly felt a reminder.

this morning I awoke to a blue-grey silk rose on my windowsill
to match her eyes; I keep it in a glass case streaked with rain
and my memory is all red-gold dragon strands falling on me, burning.

the smell of old books and desire is the greatest aphrodisiac.

THE ONGOING ADVENTURES OF GORGEOUS GRACIE

In which Gracie loses her job… but finds a friend.

Grace Fitzpatrick looked down her glasses at the student sitting in her office. It was difficult to maintain the proper distance and respect between herself and her college English students, but the prim outfits she wore and the glasses she didn't need helped. At least she hoped so. She would need all the help she could get to retain her composure in front of this muscled football jock whose gaze kept drifting to her chest. She tried to hide them as much as possible, but Grace did have unusually large breasts, and there just wasn't that much that she could do about them. She tried not to look down, hoping a button hadn't come undone. They often did.

"So, Pete, it's been a full week since I assigned that memorization and analysis to the class. It was due Thursday and you didn't show up to class. It's now Friday. Where is it?" She endeavored to look stern, but her glasses kept slipping off her elegant nose, and she had to push them up with a delicate pink-nailed finger.

"Oh, I'm sorry, Miss Fitzpatrick." He blushed sweetly. "You see, I was helping a little old lady across the street on my way to class, and a car came barreling out of nowhere and hit me. I cracked several ribs and broke an arm, so I had to miss class. I haven't been able to write, so I can't hand you the assignment, but I memorized my analysis as well as the scene… Would you like to hear it?" Pete smiled appealingly at her, the light catching his perfect teeth.

Grace was stunned. She had expected some tawdry excuse and a request for an extension. She had thought that all the bandages swathing his massive body were from a football injury. To realize how noble Pete's actions really were almost caused her to swoon. But wait… first she had to hear him recite.

"Oh. All right. Go ahead, Pete. I'm listening."

Pete sat up straight in the wooden chair, opened that wide-jawed mouth and began to recite. "Tomorrow and tomorrow and tomorrow creeps in this petty pace from day to day…" Grace was awed by the power in his voice and the obvious time and energy he had put into his presentation. She had been standing by her desk, but as he continued, she sunk down to perch on the edge, not realizing that the motion caused her cream-colored skirt to slide up her thigh, exposing a few more delectable inches. Pete continued to recite, and Grace's heart was captured in a quick flutter as she gazed at that large, firm mouth moving so... commandingly. When he finished, there was a long moment of silence.

"Very, very good, Pete. And the analysis?" This was the true test, since the boy might only have been blessed with great talent, but little brain. Grace could never truly love a man who was not as intelligent as she. He began to speak, addressing the problem of despair with what was clearly a razor-sharp mind. Grace ran her little pink tongue around her seashell lips, her heart rate beginning to climb. He cited references, proving not only that he had done his research but had understood it. Grace suddenly realized how overheated the room was, and undid the top two buttons of her blouse, opening the way for his eyes to fall on the tops of her delectable breasts. Pete continued steadfastly, moving from exposition on the historical aspects of the question to analysis of the motivations of Shakespeare in writing the piece. Grace crossed and recrossed her legs, trying to ignore the burning heat between her thighs. He finally moved to a resounding critique of the secondary sources, reaching heights never before achieved by one of her students, and Grace was lost!

She flung herself off the desk and into his lap, dropping hundreds of tiny kisses all over him as she ripped open his shirt, sending buttons flying. Her chest heaved and her own buttons flew off. Her immense breasts popped out of the brassiere that was simply incapable of restraining them and Grace grabbed Pete's head and buried his still analyzing mouth in the creamy mounds. His mouth kept moving, sending delightful shivers through her. Grace straddled him, her slim skirt sliding up stocking-clad thighs to reveal the cream lace garters that were her one indulgence. Her soft breasts pressed against Pete's hairy chest, and her fingers worked quickly to undo his pants. His stiff erection slid out smoothly, and before Pete could say historicity, her bare virgin cunt was swallowing his cock.

He pierced her in one vigorous stroke, and Grace moaned in pleasure as they began sliding smoothly in sync. Pete's mouth moved skillfully over her nipples and his fingers were somehow laced together behind her back, helping her move up and down on his lap. Her velvety cunt milked his cock, and Grace's nails dug into his powerful back under his shirt. Pete hammered into her, slamming her up and down on his rigid cock. Her first-ever orgasm came quickly, and she buried her face in his massive shoulder and bit down hard to keep from screaming as the fiery waves engulfed her. A moment later, Pete's own orgasm erupted, sending waves of cum up into her still-shuddering cunt. He let out an animal groan, momentarily unable to speak, and the two of them relaxed into a pulsating heap on the sturdy wooden chair.

It was at that moment that the Senior Faculty Member swung open the door of their shared office and walked in.

"Ms. Fitzpatrick! I am appalled!" The poor old fellow looked as if he were about to have a heart attack, and Grace momentarily regretted that it hadn't been the handsome Junior Faculty Member who had walked in. She was beginning to wonder what else she had been missing in all the years that she had kept herself untouched.

"I… can explain, sir," she said hastily.

His face turned purple with indignation, and he positively sputtered his next words. "There can be no explanations for such outrageous behavior. I shall see to it that you never teach again!" With that, he turned and stalked out of the room, leaving the sweat-soaked pair entangled on the chair.

Gracie shrugged and turned back to Pete. "Well, it doesn't look like I'll be able to give you grades for much longer… but I probably have a day or two before all the forms are filled out. I think that performance definitely rated an 'A-'; why don't we see whether you can manage an 'A'? A little louder, this time." With that, Pete enthusiastically started once more, and the sound of… voices reciting Shakespeare echoed through the hallowed halls of the College.

HYMN

It is Thursday.
I will be pagan.

Thin white shirt covers
my always naked body.

Stand in front of my mirror
and for a moment only watch
the momentary rustle in the breeze
the lifting fabric over breasts
as I
exhale.

I feel earth mother today.

Hands slipping down my ribs
to encircle waist
rising to caress a breast
carrying the shirt with them
so that a long curving expanse is revealed
to the intense gaze

hands in worship.

Swaying to no music
rhythm in the flexing of thighs
rising to support a body
on tiptoe
a leg extending
up
and up
to touch Her face

a dance of praise.

Seasweet scented waters
smoothed across the altar
of my body

incense without fire.

The burning is all inside me
in the quickening of a heart
in the tensing of muscles everywhere
in the blinding of suddenly closed eyes
in the shuddering.

And I am singing

   Gloria

as I fall.

A MORE CONGENIAL SPOT

The twins were born minutes apart, the female at 12:03, the male at 12:12. Their father hadn't been able to make the event, being on duty in the Philippines at the time. No one from the immense horde of relatives had come from their scattered homes to the Denver event, so the mother had no one to prevent her from indulging her whims. When the nurse asked her what she wanted to name the children, Mrs. Smith-Riley replied, "Guinevere and Arthur." They were doomed for life.

Both of them took after their mother in appearance, with clear, almost translucent skin, flaming hair and deep green eyes. Those ethereal good looks were to be very useful to Art, who discovered at age ten that his life-long passion was to be the theatre, his dream to be a Shakespearean actor in London. He and his sister would hide in their cluttered attic, and he would declaim monologues while she brandished a fireplace poker as a makeshift sword. Luckily for her, she quickly grew bored with the theatre, and lucky for the theatre as well, since she had all the dramatic talent of a block of wood. Gwen channeled her passion into living, living dangerously, and Art became the shy, silent type, only coming alive on stage.

Not much changed when they went to college; they just became more themselves, somehow. Freed from the restrictions and tempers of her rather arbitrary mother (their father had died ingloriously in a barroom brawl years before), Gwen went to college and raged. She'd chosen the University of Chicago, rather an odd choice; but it turned out to be a school well-suited to her brilliant mind and headstrong ways. Not a place that had many rules about its students' social lives... nor really cared if they had them at all.... It left Gwen, when she wasn't excelling in her Psychology classes, free to spend her time in lewd and lascivious pursuits.

Stories were told about her on campus, legends almost. They said that she had taken on all of Alpha Delt and lived to tell the tale, that she had seduced every TA she had... to the point where they fought to get her assigned to their section, and that she considered it a personal slight against her honor to become friends with a virgin and let him, or her, remain so.

Art lived a very different life at Northwestern. He was silent in his required classes, never speaking unless pushed, never volunteering anything. Like his sister, he had no trouble with exams, and wrote complex, witty papers on the correct way to tie up your hose in the Renaissance, and the symbolism of color in Ibsen. But he had few friends, and no lovers. In Northwestern's vibrant theatre life, he was a presence only on stage, and all attempts the female drama students made to befriend him were met only with bewilderment and flight on his part. He became more and more technically skilled, more and more passionate on stage... and far lonelier elsewhere. He told none of this to his sister, who found little time in her busy social life to visit him. So things remained until the end of their senior year.

It was June 9, 1994, their mutual day of celebration. Twenty-one today, and classes were over and graduation was imminent. Their mother would be flying into Chicago in the morning. At 8 pm the twins had only a precious few hours left to themselves. They'd wound up back at Gwen's apartment after a raucous tour of her favorite campus hotspots, such as they were. Art rarely drank, but tonight was a special occasion… birthday, coming of age, and graduation all at once. The champagne was flowing freely and he was well past the tipsy stage. At that moment, he was standing on her bed, muddy shoes and all, reciting the monologue he hoped to play in London that summer: "Tomorrow, and tomorrow, and tomorrow…" It was almost painfully appropriate.

"I think you should shut up," Gwen bellowed, over the rising chant "and get laid! You'd be a lot happier."

Art's voice suddenly cut off, and he peered at his sister from behind thin glasses and strands of hair. "And what makes you think I haven't, oh sister mine? Just because I don't trumpet my conquests to the world doesn't mean I don't have a nice piece of ass stashed away somewhere."

Gwen laughed. "Dear brother, you wouldn't know a nice piece of ass if it came up and bit you." She walked towards him, waggling a forefinger at him to emphasize her point as she said, "You…are…a…virgin. Just admit it and then we can do something about it. I have some nice friends I could introduce you to… open-minded girls with a taste for redheads. And I promise they're good in bed."

Art blushed scarlet, and suddenly lost his balance, plopping down on the bed. He quickly regained his composure, sat up, and reached for his champagne glass, downing its contents before remarking, "Well, maybe I am. A virgin." He blinked owlishly at his rapidly advancing sister, whose forefinger was now pushing his chest, so that he fell backwards on the bed. Gwen crowed in triumph! "I knew it! Little brother, you have no secrets from me. Now what would you like? A slim brunette, a curvy blond? A virgin would be hard to find, but I can guarantee you disease-free." She sat on the bed next to him, counting women on her fingertips.

"Ah, big sister, how could any maiden compare to you?" Art proclaimed hastily. "I remain chaste only because I have not yet met the woman who could compare with you. Shall I compare thee to a summer's day? Thy eyes are nothing like the sun's! Hark! The fair Ophelia! To be or not to… oof!" Art's words dissolved into laughter as his sister furiously attempted to pummel him into silence.

Gwen tickled his stomach, his armpits; she pulled off his muddy shoes to tickle his feet... and that was suddenly too much. Art grabbed her wrists and pushed her backwards across the wide bed. He fell forward against her, pinning her body beneath his own, using his weight to full advantage against the suddenly scratching, wriggling mass beneath him.

Gwen slid her wrists up, still firmly grasped in his, until she had her fingers around his throat. Her knees pressed his arms against his body, so he couldn't use them to full effect. Her fingers began to tighten. "Give it up, little brother" she panted. "You know I always won our wrestling matches."

Art couldn't quite speak, but he could still move. Suddenly he rolled heavily sideways, landing on his back with Gwen above him. In the confusion, he managed to twist away from her constraining arms, and pull her fingers away from his throat. He held her arms crucified away from her body. His long legs wrapped around hers, pinning her dangerous knees. Then he said, "The last time we wrestled was five years ago, big sister. I believe you are now in check." Art laughed up at his sister's helplessness. "What are you going to do?"

Gwen suddenly smiled an oddly wistful smile. "Mate?" she asked. With that, she tilted her head down an inch... and kissed him. 'Predictable,' was Art's one startled thought, before he lost himself in the joy of kissing those well-kissed lips. He still held her arms straight out from her body. Gwen's breasts weighed heavily against his chest through the thin fabric of her t-shirt, and her hair fell uncontrolled against his face.

If there was one thing Art had learned, it was kissing, after hours of stage kisses with cold women under hot lights. Before he had only met the semblance of passion—now passion was hitting him full force, a desert storm. The room was burning in Gwen's kisses. He was drowning in the sand.

She was writhing against him, and finally he let her hands go, uncertain what else to do. Gwen seized the opportunity, and quickly reached down to her waist, lifting herself up as she pulled off the shirt. She wasn't wearing a bra, and her soft breasts hung free in the glaring light. It was too much, somehow. Having his beloved, and beautiful, sister staring him in the face, with breasts he hadn't seen since they shared a bed in grammar school. Art reached out suddenly and turned off the bedside lamp. Asking him to do this in bright light was too much.

Before he could start thinking whether it was too much even in darkness, Gwen was pulling off his shirt as well. She muttered curses at him when he moved too slowly to help her, and was soon skinning off both their jeans. Long before he could have finished "Tomorrow and tomorrow" she had them both naked as the day they were born. Minutes apart.

"What are we doing?" Art asked her softly. Gwen didn't answer, just lowering her sweet body to his eager one. Their skin burned at the touch, yet Arthur shivered under the assault. He took her silence as his cue, and from them on silence reigned, broken only by her softly moaned encouragement, and his startled sighs.

Gwen gently directed Art whenever he seemed lost, and he took her direction flawlessly. Obviously Gwen's talent in bed was a shared family trait. Familiar hands caressed skin, sweaty bodies entwined on the mud-stained bed. They separated only briefly enough for Gwen to reach out and grab a condom from her nightstand. She thought briefly that she was quite positive she didn't want any children from this union. Then the thought was buried in long-suppressed desire. She, at least, had wanted this for a long, long time. It had just taken her a while to admit it, and a little longer to maneuver it into existence.

Much later, Art lay there humming, his sister's head cradled in his shoulder. Gwen said to him, "You sound happy, little brother. What are you humming?" Art shook his head and laughed softly. "You don't want to know" he replied. Gwen twisted her head to look up at his face. "Don't try to tell me what I want," she said. "Would you have predicted tonight?"

Art kept his memory of that first startled thought to himself, and gallantly answered, "No, though I might have dreamt of it." Gwen continued staring up at him, obviously waiting for her answer. Art laughed and gave in.

"It's from Camelot. It's the song where Arthur wins Guinevere by telling her about Camelot's scenic beauty." Gwen punched his side indignantly.

"We pledged that we would never, ever see that show!"

Art tried to fend her off, "Enough, big sister! I was auditioning for it, what could I do?" Gwen didn't seem particularly calmed by this explanation. Art continued, "If it's any consolation, I was auditioning for Arthur, and I didn't get the part."

That won a startled laugh from Guinevere. Arthur took the opportunity to lift himself up on an elbow and begin to sing to her in a low tenor, "And there is simply not, a more congenial spot, for happy-ever-aftering than here…."

Art paused suddenly, his eyes locked on her smiling face. "We can't ever do this again, you know" he said. His eyes were suddenly wistful. "I know," she replied, as she put up a hand to caress his face. "Thank you for the lesson, big sister" he said softly. Gwen suddenly laughed again, rolling around so she was seated on his stomach. "We've got at least five hours till mom gets here. I think you need a little more tutoring before I let you go."

With that, Gwen leaned down to kiss him, and Art gave up the last of his worries and kissed her back. He started humming softly… until she bit him. Then it was silence once again.

DREAMS OF A DISTANT LOVER

Dearest,

I dreamt of you last night. My dark hands slipping across pale skin in candlelight, to brush against a hardened nipple, or cup a smooth cheek. Your whispers in my ear, your hips sliding slick against mine, your hair falling soft to lightly tickle the pulse point at my throat.

There are days I think that I will die without you, that if one more moment slips past without you with me, I will fade and shrivel away, a handful of brown dust. And then I read your words, and I am a dancing dust mote, my love, basking in the shaft of sunlight that is you. And it is worth it all, every dark and dreary hour, for those sweet, foolish words you gift to me.

I long for you, my darling. For the hardness of you, the tenderness of you, the rough skin of sweaty palms tight against my hips, my waist, my breasts. I waste away for you, I melt for you, steamy and dripping and begging for you...

...for that dark skin and those tight curls, those firm or wrinkled hands, the smooth or curving belly. Are your eyes grey or blue or silver? Do not answer, I beg you. Since I will never gaze into those eyes or run my fingers through your hair, I will shape you as I choose. Tonight you will be an elven lover in my dreams, tall and slim with silver eyes and hair; tomorrow you may be a dark and swarthy charmer, or a blond boy with innocence shining out of blue eyes.

Maybe this is better than learning the truth. You can imagine me and I you, and your wife and my lover cannot be hurt by this silent, this forbidden love. No promises (foolish or not) will be broken, and we will make no new promises to each other (to be tempted to the breaking point in turn). We will be wise, and true, and do no wicked deeds we would doubtless regret.

But my heart, I'll dream of you tonight. I hope you dream of me.

LETTER FOUND NEAR A SUICIDE

This is for Maureen. This is for Maureen to tell her all the things I could not tell her. This is for Maureen O'Reilly, who lives on Elm Street, near the old church.

You have the sweetest lips I've ever seen. I wonder sometimes how many guys have kissed them, sucking hungrily at their fullness, drawing you in deeper and deeper. Many, I know. They swarm around you, bees to red honey, and you give them a taste before pulling away. A deep taste. A long, slow, rich taste. (I've hidden in the tall grasses behind the gym and watched you in the toolshed. Twice I was brave enough to stay for a while and watch as one of them kissed those full lips and large breasts.) You've had large breasts for years now, pale and slightly freckled when you lie in the sunlight with your shirt unbuttoned and your bra undone. And from the time you were ten years old you used them to tease the men. The nuns were always giving you disapproving looks. Sister Agnes actually walked over once at recess and buttoned the top button. The nuns in high school seem easier somehow.

And you were easy. Even I, who loved you, can't deny that. You were so ripe, hanging there, waiting for someone to reach up, laughing, and pull you down and you would fall willingly into his arms. (I could never watch after he'd taken off his clothes. You, I could watch naked forever, your masses of red hair sliding over your skin as you moaned and shivered. But when he took off his clothes I closed my eyes… and only listened). But you never stayed. You'd pull yourself back up into that tree and bloom again, a scarlet flower, a pomegranate, a cluster of raspberries, an apple.

Maybe cranberry suits you best. So flaming gorgeous, but sour inside. I hated you sometimes. Your easy laughter with them. Your easy smiles for them. Your easy dismissal of me. I would lie in bed on hot August nights with the fan turned on me and the sheets kicked off, my hand below my waist and my eyes focused on the sky outside the window… and I would plot revenge. Plans to drug you, and keep you tied up in my room, where I would spend hours (with you blindfolded, so you would never know whom I was) caressing that lush body, those overlarge breasts and pale skin. Plans to beat you gently, then fiercely, with my father's heaviest belt… to punish you for never noticing me enough to reject me.

Maureen, Maureen, Maureen. I could never do it. The first tear from those amber eyes and I would be lost. I am lost. Lost in my love, in my lust, in all the things that should not be but are.

Perhaps you will truly hate me after this. Perhaps this letter will make your life miserable… depending on who finds it first, out on the front steps of the school. The pills are starting to work… I'm getting very sleepy, and it's hard to write. I hope they don't publish it. Whoever reads this first - don't send it to the paper. Don't tell the whole town. I just want the school to know. And Maureen. That I loved her for the last three years. Maureen, maybe you can carry my love with you. You don't need to sleep with all those men. Then again, if you stopped, you wouldn't be you.

Sincerely,

Caroline Tilden

Honor Student, Class Vice President

UNABASHED PAEAN

Daily new crocuses push their way through the moist soil, and
A fall of ivory petals sheathes the swooping vine-like
Feathered branches of the old tree along the walk. Song
Fills my throat and aches to burst free; villanelles and
Odes dance in my brain, whispering, chanting spring.
Do you feel it, my dears? Do you feel the blood racing
Its sudden course? If you do, you will find a sweet body and
Lay yourselves down in the grass amid crushed daffodils,
Singing silently with every inch of sun-touched skin.

JAPANESE GARDEN

If you've ever been to Chicago, and are at all the museum-going type, you've probably been to the Museum of Science and Industry. It's worth seeing, with the Omnimax 360-degree theatre, the over-priced coal mine ride, and the tons of cool techno gizmos. If you're anything like me, you can't resist the glass globe with the sparks that reach out to caress your hand, or the computer quizzes. But the best thing about it in 1989 was that it was still free. Only a ten-minute walk from my dorm, it was irresistible during those rare weeks of Indian summer, when it was warm and humid enough that you desperately wanted to be naked, or at least outside by the lake.

And it was a good place to go kill an afternoon with a new boyfriend.

Dean was scum. Or at least he had a totally scummy side, but I didn't find that out till many months later. In early October I was a freshman in college and terribly in love. In love with a poor Physics sophomore, who couldn't afford dinner and roses but could kiss better than anyone I'd kissed before. That wasn't saying much then, but he could kiss better than almost anyone I've kissed since, and that *is* saying something. A funny-looking guy over a foot taller than me, with long, greasy hair and wretched taste in T-shirts. I think he was wearing the shirt with fake bird droppings that day, and cut-off jeans and new sneakers his mom had sent. And sparks were flying. We couldn't keep our hands off each other. Luckily for us, we didn't have to try very hard.

It was evening, and we had been duly kicked out of the museum at 4:00. Now if you're only a casual visitor to Chicago, you've probably heard about the Museum of Science and Industry, but you've probably never seen the small pond nearby where you can go paddleboating (so they say—I've never seen it myself), or the Japanese garden around the back. I'm not sure why they call it a Japanese garden, which I always though was a rather spare arrangement of sand and stones in a box not much bigger than a dining table. This place was lush. It had winding paths and strange trees—large trees, not bonsai. Mostly, it had little secluded nooks, and statues. I don't remember anything about the statues now… whether they were Greek, or Indian, or even Japanese. But the statues are important. Remember them.

So we had been kicked out of the museum, and had found our way to the garden. We'd only been going out a month. We were both virgins at the time, not surprising for the type of students who found their way to the University of Chicago, and I at least didn't plan to rush things any. I may have been in love, but I had also been a good Catholic girl for far too many years, and some of that had to rub off.

I've heard that the Catholic girls are the wildest once they finally get going. Worked for me, anyway. So back then I wasn't having intercourse, but boy, were we doing everything but.

Kissing and fondling was where it started, and it generally ended with us mostly undressed. Once we'd fallen asleep naked in my tiny dorm room in the middle of the afternoon, and when my roommates came home and fiddled with the door, Dean rolled over me, so they only saw his slightly hairy butt before hurriedly backing out into the hallway and hollering at us to *please* get dressed. He had a gallant streak in him—one of the things I loved about him, although looking back, I certainly exaggerated the size of it. Typical with old lovers, I suppose. They somehow seem kinder, more romantic, more attractive, and have bigger penises… until you decide to call them up, just to see how they're doing, and are reminded of just how boring they actually were, and just why you were glad they broke it off. Before *you* had to.

But at that point, I had no vast experience of ex-lovers to compare him to, and Dean seemed like heaven itself. His hands sliding under my white t-shirt, to reach in back with already-practiced fingers and unhook the over-small bra, somehow slipping it off me and dropping it in the grass. His mouth on mine as we fell to the ground and rolled around, trying to be quiet, although there was no sound but us and the cars on Lake Shore Drive. His tongue was long, and the memory of it can still occasionally bring a flush of heat to my skin. We humped, fully clothed, in the itchy grass, my hands with their bitten nails digging into the back of his T-shirt, his hands in my still-short hair, pulling it back so he could leave dark, hot hickies on my neck while his chest pressed my breasts back into my ribs, and my ribs into the ground. My legs were wrapped around one of his, the rising musky scent seeped through my thin skirt and combined with sweat and the smell of Tide that permeated his clothing, until it was hard to breathe from that and his weight. And I must have whimpered, because it was suddenly too much, and he was standing up and hauling me with him, no doubt planning to go back to the dorms where we could strip and finish this properly.

Only I wasn't willing to wait that long, and I pulled him to me, grabbing the back of his head and pulling him down to my level so we could keep kissing, because at that moment, I wanted nothing more than to kiss him until he or I burst. He groaned softly then, and pushed me back against one of the large stone statues, its solid cool bulk a shock after all that heat. Then suddenly, his hands were under my skirt, pulling off the white cotton underwear I still wore back then. I lifted each leg so he could remove it, at that point not caring that we were in a public garden, and that at any moment the City of Chicago police might come and take us away for indecent exposure, or disturbing the peace.

Dean paused a minute, then slipped his hands under my ass and lifted me up, startling me, then put me down to rest on a ledge of the statue. It had hands, you see, cold smooth hands that jutted out in front, just at the level of his head. It was a huge statue, and perched on that pair of hands, I was taller than I'd been since I was a small child perched on a friendly adult's shoulders. He'd pushed the short black skirt I'd borrowed from a roommate's friend out of the way as he set me down, and I worried briefly about the hordes of outdoor germs on the cold stone. I didn't worry long, though, because at this level it only took a second for him to push the front of my skirt out of the way as well, and all he had to do was lean forward and start licking as if his life depended on it. Or mine. I almost screamed right then, arching under his touch. My arms were behind me, so my hands could help maintain my precarious balance, and my legs were wrapped around his head as he licked and sucked and slid fingers in and out of me, until I was shaking and quietly begging...

And he started doing something, I still don't know what, and I was suddenly coming so hard, so fast, that I lost all balance and slid right off the statue, falling into him and crashing to the ground. And it was then that we heard voices coming towards us. He grabbed my underwear and bra and stuffed it in a pocket, and pulled me to my feet, both of us still dizzy. And we ran.

I don't think we ever made it back to the dorm that fast again, or were ever quite so glad that his roommate wasn't home. We locked the door and tore off clothes and fell on each other with fingers and slick skin and eager tongue... and I'm still amazed that it took a whole three months before we got around to having intercourse.

Amazing the power of inhibitions. And the power and excitement that comes of ignoring them.

RENEWAL

It has been a long long time since I have known
such delights. Summer's close about us,
with sluggish days that beg for storing sleep. And yet,
a rain-swift rush of blood cries out that it must be spring.
And all the turning leaves and orange blossoms must proclaim
that life, not death, has sovereignty this day.

I am a garden, love, run wild and fertile under your caress.
No gardener could better train these creeping vines
and scattered blooms. So wander in my pathways for awhile,
your fingers tracing waterfalls along a shaking soil.
And we will surge and rush and come again to silence—
there is no sweeter sorcery on this earth.

RADHIKA AND MATTHEW

She is stunning in a white and gold sari, a princess more beautiful than any in the German fairy tales. White suits her far better than it could have any of the those milksop blond maidens. She seems cool and calm, despite the August heat. His palms sweat in the white New England church, his pale skin incongruous against the sea of brown faces. All he thinks as he breathes is what a shame that custom binds her hair, studded with carnations and gold.

They're tying the heavy thali around her neck, the crimson-clad mother stepping forward to help the trembling groom. Mrs. Annadurai was born and raised in a village near Jaffna, and believes in her heart that it would be a very bad sign if the groom dropped the wedding necklace, though she'd never admit it even to her Indian friends. And then they exchange the rings, and raise their voices in hymn. Most of the church is silent, filled with Muslim and Hindu neighbors.

He remembers suddenly, sharply, the way she falls asleep immediately after sex, unlike the few other women he'd known. She curls trusting into a slightly flabby shoulder, and he rocks her gently, unbelieving of his luck. The scent of sandalwood clings to her skin, long after the incense has burned away. She burned it often in those days, whenever she had been thinking about the rift between herself and her parents.

They're filing out now, having skipped the traditional kiss, to the discomfort of the few white faces in the crimson-flowered church. Groom and bride, hand in hand. And Radhika is smiling, though perhaps looking a little nervous; standard for the bride. Despite her college experiences with men, she has, after all, never been married before. Her plump parents, however, show no such restraint in their smiles.

When he first met her parents, they were so polite. Surprisingly charming in person, these New England doctors. No hint in their eyes of the hours screaming over the phone, as Radhika tried, over and over, to reconcile them to him and to her life. Face, what he'd once thought an East Asian concept, was terribly important here. Though Mrs. Annadurai had managed to avoid shaking his hand then.

Radhika's mother does not hesitate to shake it now, and the triumphant glow of her face as he walks down the receiving line twists the bitterness inside him. Even drowning out the beauty of Radhika's sad and private smile, as he wonders what he could have done, should have done to keep her. Bitterest of all is that he suspects he could have done nothing at all to change her mind.

Charming to the end, they'd even invited him to the wedding.

YOU ARE CORDIALLY INVITED
TO THE WEDDING OF

RADHIKA MARIE ANNADURAI
AND
MATTHEW ARAVINDEN KONESWARAN

LETTER

> Almost eleven—you will be up for hours still
> but I will sleep soon.

Sorry you are away.

> I doubt you'll get home in time to talk or touch
> which is a shame because I want to fuck you to absolution
> or oblivion.
> Whichever comes first.

Funny how much you hate sunlight,
because when I image you it is almost always in terms of light.
White gold as sunlight touches the fine hairs on your arm… realms of light
and shadow in a dimly lit room caress the place
where shoulder meets neck in a delicate hollow begging to be kissed.

> I enjoyed watching tv tonight, but I would have enjoyed
> not watching it with you better.

We should go to New England and I could push you down into a prickly-
carpet of autumn leaves and pine needles.
When we finally rose, scent of crushed pine would hang heavy in the air
and I would not tell you about the mantle of fire-leaf fragments in gold
hair.

> You are so golden. Blond is nowhere near enough a word.

Talking about intensity with an old lover tonight I suddenly
remembered walking with you once and feeling so helpless as I told
myself that I should just shut up and go away and make your life a little
simpler. And then you turned to me and said such things that I was convinced that I was a fool sometimes.

> Happy enough to cry. For a change.

I love the way you've been kissing my neck lately. I think sometime soon,
when I'm very awake and it's either not late at night or so late that I've
moved past being tired, I would like to spend a very long time kissing your
sweet body. On and on until you plead exhaustion.

> Teach me to make chocolate mousse and we will spend a guilty
> afternoon on pleasure, remembering tiramisu and raspberry
> liqueur in chocolate on pale skins with sweet smiles
> and frighteningly open hearts.

Tell me again that you love me
and that this letter is not too much an imposition.

    I have this terrible temptation to turn this into a poem.

(for Kevin)

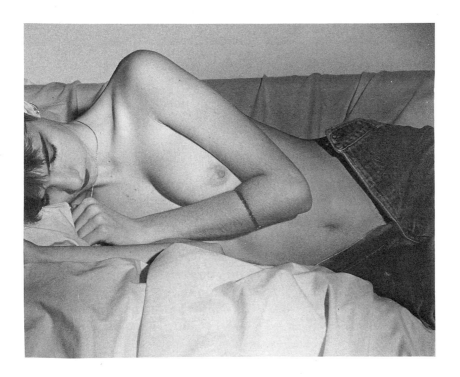

THE DEVOURING NIGHT

The bride-to-be of Gamilah, twelfth prince of that name, lord of the richest province in all of Ranek, was alone in her tower room. It was her first moment alone in twelve days, and she cherished it, holding it to her like a gift far more precious than the dozen purebred peacocks in the courtyard or the teardrop ruby hanging at her throat. Twelve days of feasting; twelve last days of innocence. And tonight, oh tonight would be the marriage feast, and the prince, her lord, would claim her as his own. Perhaps if she drank enough wine, she could forget that tonight she would become his bride. She could lose herself in wine and music and poetry, at this final feast.

"Sharmi?" Her servant stepped into the room, not bothering to announce her presence. They had gone beyond formality long ago; Veena was more of an aunt to Sharmi than a servant. Still, they were no longer safely home.

"'Princess Sharmila', Veena. And you must announce yourself." Sharmila's tone was gently chiding, with no real force to it. If Veena hadn't been exhausted by the twelve days of feasting and ritual, she would have been the one making the correction, not Sharmila.

"My apologies, my princess." Veena ducked her greying head abashedly. "But it's almost time."

"I'm ready." Sharmila gathered the final folds of her crimson and gold-shot silk wedding sari in her arm, and stood tall for Veena's inspection. Her oiled and perfumed hair hung past her hips like a midnight waterfall, and the rich gold of her dowry rested heavy on wrists and ears and neck.

"You look lovely, princess. You'll make a perfect bride for... him." Veena had hesitated before naming the prince, and Sharmila knew that her servant harbored the same doubts about this new lord. He was so old, so stern. Yet, as her mother had told her, marriage had its compensations. She had no choice in the matter in any case. For now... it was her wedding day.

***

She will come back in her body
She will desire him like sin
She will desire him like virtue

The poet's voice rose and fell, climbing and receding like the tides. The prince sat on the high platform, ensconced in cushions like a great elephant at rest, his head nodding approval at what seemed a perfect wedding poem. But as the poet's voice continued, Sharmila trembled.

> In some unknown place
> In an unknown room
> She will make love to him in her thoughts...

The poet was a lean man, a hungry man. Poets were many in Ranek, and competition was fierce for court favor. The Queen in her palace had the best of them, but each of the lesser princes could boast four or five court poets, who lived lives of luxury far beyond that of the common bard. They had come from the country and the cities to court her favor, in the hope that she might bear some influence with her lord and win them a post in his court. This one had dressed in sober black, rather than the peacock hues of his comrades, a slim ebony blade in a night of brilliant fireworks. His eyes were locked on hers, and she could not tear her gaze away. She had seen him before, this poet. He was one among many who flattered and praised her, eyes burning. She had taken little notice of him, except to note that he was perhaps somewhat handsomer than most. But she had been surrounded by beauty since birth, and he was nothing. A poet. But now his words grew dangerous. The soft flowers that fell from his lips had turned to jewels, to knives. If he was not very careful, they would cut him.

> She will desire him
> Like a kind of dream...

When the poet finished reciting the famous words of Gagan, the prince nodded his approval. Sharmila breathed easier, and began to once again pick at her dish of cucumber and rose water, gathering her courage for the coming night. But then he began again.

"My prince. I offer a humble poem of my own working. May you smile upon it."

With the first lines, terror gripped Sharmila. She carefully pushed away her dish, and turned, to fix her smile upon the prince. He smiled down at her, and so they continued for the length of the poem.

> My love is sweet as jasmine,

Blooming only at night.
She climbs garden walls
Beneath my eyes;
Opens only to my touch.
My love is bright as starlight,
Surrounded by the dark.
She cannot be smothered
By the devouring night;
My skin burns, fired by her touch.

When it ended, the poet waited, silent. The prince absent-mindedly threw a gold ring to the man, and then bent to kiss his princess. The poet bowed, and turned away.

The rest of the evening passed in a golden haze for Sharmila. She felt feverish, and as the sandalwood and jasmine incense mingled in the overheated room, the princess feared she would faint. Dish after dish was paraded before her; cool sherbets and tall yoghurt drinks alternating with curried vegetables and spiced meats. She barely touched them, until the prince could not help but notice.

"You are not eating, my dear."

"The excitement is too much for me, my lord. It has been a long twelve days of feasting."

"I, too, long for the day to be over, my love. Come. You must try this at least. I ordered it especially to tempt your appetite." The prince clapped his hands, and the cook came forward with a small covered dish. The prince removed the golden lid to reveal another dish of spiced meat, unusual only in its size. "It is small, I know, but the beast it comes from does not have a mighty heart. It is said to be most tender, though. Will you not try it?"

Sharmila tentatively tasted the dish, and as the delicately flavored sauce melted on her tongue, she realized that she was indeed hungry once more. She reached towards the dish, and the cook deftly slipped the contents of the dish onto her plate before vanishing into the kitchen. The prince smiled as he watched her eat voraciously, contenting himself with a glass of crimson wine. When she finished, he said, "May your appetite for that dish be a good omen for our marriage; may all your appetites flourish within it." Sharmila blushed, then shivered as he leaned forward to kiss her again. Despite his kindness, she felt nothing but revulsion at his touch, and thought with longing of the dark poet, slender as a blade.

When the last rays of the setting sun cast their dim glow over the room, Am'kele's priest spoke the final words, sealing them together as husband and wife. Then the prince took Sharmila's hand in his, and they walked through the garden to her tower, under the light of hanging oil lamps and the rising moon.

It was hours later when she arose from the bed. She gathered her white gown around her, and crossed to stand by the window. The moon hid behind clouds, but the light of stars caressed her battered body, and her eyes were dark pools as she gazed out upon the garden far below.

"Looking for your poet, my wife?"

Sharmila spun around, her gasp betraying her as surely as a murmured assent. The prince lounged among the pillows, a bitter smile lighting his face. "You will not find him in the garden. That dish you found so tasty, that you devoured like the little beast you are? It was his heart. They cut it from him, still beating, and basted it with his blood. Have a care for your poets and courtiers, my wife. I do not take kindly to those who desire the beauty that is mine."

"He was only a poet, my lord." Her voice cracked. "I did not even know his name. We had not betrayed you!"

The prince growled, low in his throat. "Can you swear you had not thought of it? Swear that, wife, and I will believe you. But I know you cannot, for women are beasts, willingly spreading their legs for any prince or poet who comes by. Can you deny it?"

Sharmila was silent a long moment. Perhaps she had consoled herself with thoughts of a midnight tryst, of sweet moments stolen from a prisoned life. "Whatever I thought, I have not done, and neither had that poor poet. You are the true beast among us." Her hands were clenched on the window sill, her painted nails cracked and digging into stone.

"Beast I may be, wife. But I am your husband still, and you had best get used to it." He rose then, and began to cross the room towards Sharmila. His heavy bulk moved toward her slender frame, and for a moment it seemed that she would be smothered beneath him. Then she stepped up into the window, silhouetted by the starlight, and spoke again.

"I am not used to living caged, my lord." She laughed softly, bitterly. "I fear I would not thrive in such a case, and such beauty as I have should all be ruined. Perhaps you should remember me as I am; a somewhat battered bride, but with the taste of the sweetest meal I've ever had still upon my tongue." With that, she stepped out the tower window, and was gone.

***

She will come back in her body…

The Raneki believe in reincarnation. When the poets tell the tale of Sharmila Avasthi, they say that she was reborn into her House generations later, and eventually went to her poet as his bride. They say she always had a love of gardens, and a passion for the night. It was she who ordered the colors of her House changed to black and silver; night and starlight. None can say what the truth of the matter is, but one thing remains true, even unto the present day. On the night of Sharmila's leap from the tower, the poets deserted Gamilah province. The bards and minstrels and songsters went with them, and not a one has returned, for memory of her.

COMPOSITION IN CREAM AND CHOCOLATE

You walk into the small room with its vaulting ceiling. The lights dim automatically as you take your seat in the comfortable green chair. A blond man walks across the darkened stage, and a spotlight hits his face, casting sharp shadows across its pale lines. He smiles at you, the sole patron of this most elegant club tonight.

"A private show?" he asks. You nod, waiting for him to announce the act. His smile deepens, as he steps back, gesturing grandly at the room around you. "Welcome to Wench Works! Tonight for your entertainment and...pleasure...we have a very special performance. Please sit back, have a drink, and enjoy the show!"

The spotlight abruptly cuts off, and the man disappears into sudden darkness. Your eyes take a moment to adjust, and even when they do the stage appears black. Music swells in the background, an invisible orchestra playing an unusual theme. It is slow, controlled, and somehow subtly erotic. It leaves you with the impression of massive power, channeled into a thing of great beauty, and trails off tantalizingly, unfinished.

A golden spotlight hits the bare stage, near the front. It moves slowly backwards, up the center stage, and focuses on a pair of black boots. Ever-so-faintly, you can make out silver tracery on the boots as your eye, and the spotlight, follows them upwards. The spot outlines tight black pants, clinging to clearly-defined muscles in long, lean legs. The pants hide nothing. They caress strong thighs and narrow hips before disappearing under a midnight blue silk shirt.

The shirt is very thin and slides gently in the breeze from the ceiling fan, turning lazily on this hot night. You are sweating as you follow the light, and a drop of perspiration slides down your collarbone to fall into the crevice between your breasts. You almost regret wearing black tonight, as even a light chiffon dress is too hot in this small room. You take a drink from the glass on the table, tipping your head back as the cool liquid slips down your throat, careful to keep your eyes on the stage.

The spotlight has paused, as if waiting for you to put down your glass, and as you do so, it starts moving upwards again, and the music returns softly. It thrums a gentle counterpoint as the light plays over a dancer's body. There is little mass here, but there is power in the shoulders, in the chest, in the arms. The silk shirt is buttoned all the way to the top, and a loose black vest hangs over it, also buttoned. You feel sorry for the man in all of the layers, and feel a desire to relieve his... discomfort. You restrain yourself though, and your only movement now is your foot tapping in time to the music.

The light refuses to move above his neck, though it expands down to include his entire body, a sword of midnight and black lit by the golden glow. His hands slowly rise from his sides to the top button of the black vest, which is also traced in silver. He starts to unbutton the vest, oddly caressing each button, sliding his hands up and around, his fingertips circling before he tugs gently at the buttonhole.

Your nipples are growing hard as you watch him, pressing through the fragile fabric despite the heat of the room. You re-cross your legs, feeling the chiffon damp against your thighs, folds of fabric trapped between your legs. You continue to tap to the music, the motion rubbing one leg against the other in a slow, steady rhythm.

He does all three buttons that way, slowly teasing. He shrugs out of the vest in one smooth, practiced motion, leaving it to pool behind him on the floor. He reaches to undo the top button of the silk shirt, and freezes as you lift your hand. Evidently, he can see you clearly, even if you can't see his face. You crook a finger and beckon him towards you. He comes.

He walks slowly off the stage, disappearing for a moment into unlit darkness. The music begins to increase in tempo, a slight change that perhaps only a musician would catch. Or someone concentrating very, very hard. The room is still black.

Then the flicker of candlelight coming towards you. A tall, white candle, welcome against the darkness. He walks around the circular room, lighting similar white candles hung in wall sconces. He then brings his to you, and places it on the table near your glass. He stands silent, awaiting your pleasure.

You can finally see his face, barely lit by candlelight. Pale blue eyes glow out of a pale face to match. Silken blond hair falls forward, obscuring one eye. You reach up to brush the hair aside, coming half way out of your chair. He catches your wrist, smiling, and shakes a silent 'no'. He releases your hand and you let it fall as you sit back down. You slide down the silk shirt, damp in the heat, pressing your small hand against his skin through the thin fabric.

You slide it further, to the bulge in the tight black pants, cupping your hand around quickly hardening flesh. You run your fingers up and down his inner thigh, moving up to caress his balls, then between his legs to squeeze a firm buttock. He stands motionless throughout and only because he is so close can you hear his quickened breath above the music.

You then lean forward and gently breathe on that space just inside his hip. Reaching out with your tongue, you trace a path to his now hard cock, nibbling gently through the fabric. Your hand between his legs pulls him closer and he sways forward, extending one hand to the table for support.

The other finds its way to your hair and wraps itself in long, black waves, pulling your head closer as well.

You give him one more kiss and pull away, though. His hand in your hair is still, exerting no force. You stand up, coming only to his chest, and deliberately begin to undo buttons. One, two, three, four... using that same terribly slow movement that he taught to you from the stage. His chest is smooth, as you prefer, almost hairless. You rub your cheek against it as you continue to undo buttons. Five, six, seven... and eight. Finished, you reach up and slip the shirt off his shoulders. It slides off, until caught at the wrists. You hadn't undone the buttons at the cuffs, and he is trapped within the shirt. You leave him that way.

You begin to drop tiny kisses on his skin, following a long, slow path down one arm. You nip gently at the elbow as he tries to remain still, and spend an endless time licking and sucking each finger of his left hand. You enjoy this immensely, circling the tips with your tongue, biting very gently with your teeth, humming in the back of your throat in time to the swelling music.

You then let go of his hand and return to his white body. You pause to mark him, sucking hard at the tender juncture of neck and collarbone until a violent red mark appears. You pull back to admire your work, then pull your fingernails down his chest, just hard enough to leave clear red lines, beautiful against the white skin. You look back up at him, and he is smiling.

You go back to dropping kisses down his body, curving over his chest, sliding down his stomach, your tongue licking at the sweat coating his skin. You nibble at his ribs, and his right hand, still caught in your hair, pulls you sharply away. Your head is pulled back so you are forced to look at him briefly. He shakes his head again. You nod in agreement and he relaxes his grip.

Now your fingers undo the button on his pants and unzip them. He wears nothing underneath, and his cock is caught against one side. You reach in with your right hand and grasp it firmly, pulling it out of its prison and into the open air.

The air in the room is cooler now. A cold breeze is blowing from up in the rafters, and the sweat is cooling quickly on your body, chilling your skin. You move closer to him and kneel down, your hair falling around you. You are an elegant line of black, your body silhouetted in candlelight.

You unlace his boots quickly, growing impatient. He lifts each leg so you can pull off the boots and toss them under the table. Black socks go too, and it only takes a moment for you to reach up and pull down the black pants, unpeeling them from his muscled legs. He steps out of those as well, and now stands clad only in the blue silk hanging from his wrists, one hand still entangled in your hair.

He is beautiful in the candlelight, glowing lion-gold. You rise to your feet again, and stand before him, still fully dressed yourself. You shiver in the growing cold, and lean forward to press a chaste kiss on warm lips... but the kiss doesn't remain chaste for long. He captures your mouth in his, and the kiss turns almost violent. His tongue probes your mouth, exploring, as his hands clasp your waist and pull you towards him.

He cannot embrace you fully with his arms constrained, but his fingers hold you firmly, the thin chiffon no barrier as strong hands slide down your hips to cup your thighs and pull you to him. His warmth is welcome against the cold of the room. His eyes glow pale blue in the candlelight.

You suddenly notice the music crescendoing, and you are somehow sinking down to the lushly carpeted floor, underneath him. He is kissing you fiercely now, and you moan, arching up to meet him as his fingers dig into your buttocks. There is the faint sound of fabric tearing and his arms are suddenly sliding up your curving back, tangling once more in your hair, scratching down the dark brown skin covering your spine.

Your own arms are wrapped around his at first, but as he pulls down the straps of the black dress, you relax your arms and slip them free, curving up so he can pull down the top of the dress. He quickly unsnaps the front of your lace bra, freeing your breasts into the chill of the room, their dark nipples firm and erect in the bracing cold, and your own heat. He drops one last quick kiss on your lips, and then begins to tease your nipples with his tongue, tracing inward spirals on your breast until he has almost reached the nipple and then suddenly changing to the other breast, leaving you gasping.

You only tolerate this for a few minutes before you reach up and pull his head towards you, whimpering softly as you do so. You'll never know whether it was the whimper or your movement that caused him to take pity on you, but soon his mouth is warm and wet against your right nipple, sucking and pulling and nibbling gently while he rolls the left in practiced fingers.

He then begins to nibble the skin of your stomach, your ribs, pushing the dress down until it just covers your hips and he can taste the salty skin near your hipbones. Your moans are almost covered by the rising music. You are writhing beneath him now, begging under your breath for him to please fuck you now, sliding your legs down his sides so the chiffon rides high on your thighs. The fabric inches upward until you can finally rub your cunt against his skin, bare flesh against flesh.

At that he seems to break, and lifts his head from your body long enough to look at you one more time. Then he slides his hands down and at first he seems to be removing your dress but he's actually sliding it up and lifting you higher and he is suddenly plunging in you, his long hard cock enveloped in your warm wetness. The music swells to a grand crescendo now, and the room is echoing as he moves back and forth inside you. Your legs wrap around him and you pull him closer, using his body to pull yourself deeper and harder against him.

And you are splitting inside and out and you are both sweating now despite the cold, your slick bodies sliding against each other and your long black hair sprayed out behind you like a fan against the dark green carpet. He bends down once more to a breast and bites and your fingers are digging deep into his shoulders. Your legs are clenched tight against his body trying to hold him still but he is too far gone for that and pounds deeper and faster and you are suddenly screaming above the music and you are both curving into a sudden frozen arc and the spotlight suddenly comes down on you both, blinding white. As you collapse into a pile of cream and chocolate skin, limbs wrapped around each other, his head resting on your shoulder, a solo flute arpeggios its way up into ending.

As the spotlight fades to black, restrained clapping is heard from the gallery up in the rafters. The clapping swells as more of the audience joins in, until the room is thundering with applause. You relax, finally satisfied.

ORANGE AFTER MIDNIGHT

only Chicago could have a fucking orange sky
formed of antique lampposts and
framed by fake Gothic buildings

sere grass where once, hours past midnight,
sky still orange
we regretted cold and fading inhibitions that
prevented love to match the sky
on manicured lawns

CHANTAL

She still doesn't know.

***

Chantal sits cross-legged on my futon, leaning back against the blue cushions. She hugs my stuffed lion close. Its golden fur glows in the light of my single working lamp, blending into her honey-brown skin. Her skin is a legacy of her despised mother, the fashion model. She isn't as gorgeous as her mother had been, and she isn't looking her best at the moment, tears running down her face, dressed in rumpled clothing she's slept in for two days, but she's still quite beautiful. Not that I'm objective.

I'm trying to listen to her telling me again just how much she'd loved Jeff, but even the gallon of chocolate ice cream before us is starting to lose its appeal as I listen to the story for the hundredth time, in yet another variation. She's done this before. Fallen in love, realized she had picked a jerk, dumped him or been dumped. Over and over, always with the wrong guy. I'd started to wonder if she might really be a lesbian.

We'd discussed it before, since I'd come out to her years ago, but she'd always denied the possibility and changed the topic. She'd started avoiding my touch then too, giving brief hugs on greeting and parting and sitting much farther away than she had before. Right now I'm regretting having a full-size futon, large enough that she can easily sit out of reach. I'd have to lean way over before I could run my fingers over those impossibly long brown legs, curving down her calf to cup her foot in my small hands, gently rubbing her toes. She starts sniffling again, and I hand her another tissue.

The doorbell rings. She looks up helplessly.

"Don't worry, Chantal. I'll get rid of whoever it is. Just hang on a sec." Her sniffle is quickly smothered in tissues.

"Who is it?"

"Pizza delivery."

"We didn't order any."

"Hey, I got your pizza right here."

The voice is muffled by the intercom. "I'd better go down," I tell her. Huddled there in her huge green flannel shirt, bleached blond hair falling across her face, she is so much a child.

Down the half flight of stairs, the man in the crisp white shirt stands holding a pizza, having come through our broken security doors. He holds out the pizza box. I reach out; he drops the box and is suddenly up the stairs, shoving me up against the crumbling plaster wall of the stairwell. I am almost falling onto him. I tense, then feel the prick of a knife through my black t-shirt. It is uncomfortably cold against my rib.

"Christ!" explodes unbidden from my throat, my voice rising dangerously. "What the fuck are you…"

"Shut up, you stupid bitch." he says, deceptively calm, in a voice pitched to carry through my open door. I can tell he is nervous. The knife trembles against me, and I am terrified of what is happening here in this now unfriendly building. This scene has gone out of control, and I no longer know what he, or I, will do. We enter my apartment, and he swings the door closed with his foot, not bothering to turn the lock.

Chantal has risen from the futon and stands framed in a halo of flickering light. That lamp has never been reliable, and in this uncertain moment it flickers in and out.

"Not a sound, bitch." he warns. "If the neighbors hear anything unpleasant, that's it for your girlfriend."

Chantal sinks down onto rumpled blue blankets, a moan caught in her butterfly mouth and frightened eyes locked on the glint of bright steel against black cotton. I feel a sharp pain where the knife point lies poised against me, but it is impossible to tell if I am actually bleeding against the black.

"Strip." he orders her, an unnerving thread of excitement clear in the tremor of his voice.

She shakes her head mutely in protest, wrapping her arms tight around her golden body. She must not know how that motion pulls the shirt taut against full breasts, how it pulls the fabric sliding up her legs, baring even more tawny thigh. I catch my breath at the sight, and am brought back to reality only by the lifting of the knife point from my ribs.

Just as I start to shift away he slides a tightly-muscled arm across my throat, pulling me back. He has lifted the knife only to bring it to my throat, and I freeze. He slowly slides the knife down the front of my top, slicing it cleanly in half, leaving the fabric to flap aimlessly in the wind of the creaking fan. Small dark breasts have fallen free, nipples hard with fear, and the cold breeze, and excitement. I am wearing only black cotton shorts now, and I cannot help but think how beautiful he and I must look, black against his white shirt and pants, brown curls so oddly similar. He looks like my brother, I suddenly think, and then must struggle down dangerous laughter. My nerves are being stretched far too taut.

He lifts the blade up to a breast and I am truly frozen now as he holds the knife point a fraction of an inch away from tender skin. He looks at Chantal.

"Strip." If before his voice was nervous with excitement, it is now implacable. It would take someone far braver than she to resist. She slowly begins to unbutton the oversized shirt. He is not content with the flannel slowly slipping from her shoulders.

"Stand and strip." he says, and she obeys almost silently, muffling the whimpers deep in her throat. Endless moments later she has unbuttoned the last button and the shirt falls unheeded to the floor. My gaze slips back and forth between her, (never before has she seemed so beautiful), and the possessive wanting in his eyes. "Come here." he says. At that I stiffen even more, wanting to slap that look from his face, that purr from his voice.

Her hands flutter up and down her body as she walks toward us, futilely attempting to preserve some shred of modesty, of dignity. It is useless. She is too fragile to stand up against this, and her welling tears provoke a growing rage within me. She stops, shivering in the direct wind from the ceiling fan.

His knife hand suddenly drops away from my breast, although his left arm is still rigid against my throat. He is fumbling with the zipper on his pants, finally dropping them to lie puddled on the floor around his feet. He wears no underwear, and his erection pokes out from his shirttails, pressing against my thigh. He smells of soap.

"On your knees, bitch." he says to her, the hunger clear in the hoarseness of his voice. "Suck me off."

And I can't take anymore. I jerk sideways, pulling free. His knife hand comes up quickly though, and his other hand swings in a wide grab for Chantal, only to be blocked as I step calmly in front of it.

"No." I say, the words dry in my throat as I strive to make my voice as seductive as possible. "Please" as I slide to my knees in front of him, "let me." My eyes are locked on his, and I fervently hope that he can see in them that he has pushed me far enough, farther than is safe for any of us. I am all too aware of Chantal's gasp behind me, the only sound she has let herself make, and of her skin inches away from mine. I wait for his response, unable to read past desire in deep brown eyes.

He stares in silence for long seconds, knife poised. He looks me over slowly, insolently, and I will myself not to stiffen against his intrusive gaze. Finally he nods, silently. I lean forward and run my tongue down his stiff erection. It has been many years since I last did this, but some things you remember. I trace small, lazy circles around the shaft. I feel the pulse beat-

ing in him, as the salty fluid rises. I tease the head with flicking tongue until the growing fever in the eyes I have not dared glance away from warns
me that teasing will not be permitted for long. I suddenly realize that I find
this man beautiful after all, and if he hadn't had a knife to my throat I
might have wanted this as much as he did. I begin to tremble.

It is quickly over, and I swallow carefully. I wait, kneeling in front of
him, holding his eyes with mine once more, willing him not to look away,
not to glance at Chantal. He seems to read my desire. His next words are
addressed solely to me, "Strip. Lie down." He seems to disregard Chantal,
though his body is still tight. I do not think I can get the knife away. I rise
obediently, and quickly step out of the black shorts, not wanting them to
be torn as well. Some part of my mind must still believe that we will survive
this.

I lie down on the futon, pushing aside blue blankets to create a clear
space in the center, baring the dark green sheets. I stretch lazily, offering
my body up for him to drink deep. My eyes are focused on his face, on the
raw desire battling with some indefinable thought. I doubt I could look
away if I wanted to. Some tiny detached part of me wants desperately to
photograph his face. Portrait of a rapist. I am shattering into a hundred different elements, held together only by the need to protect.

His free hand is suddenly on Chantal's shoulder, twisting her cruelly
around, off-balance. Then the hilt of the knife is shoved into the small of
her back, and she falls onto me. I voice a wordless protest, but she falls silent, curving so as not to hit too hard. Even in this she is graceful. Then he
speaks.

"Go on, bitch. Fuck her. I want to watch you sluts fucking each other
on your nice, clean sheets. Eat her, you dirty slut!" His voice rises higher
and higher, and I wonder if perhaps the neighbors will hear. Doubtful - the
walls are not that thin. Chantal is shaking her head at the stream of invec-
tive, terror blossoming. And suddenly I reach up and hold her face still in
my hands, my eyes promising her that it will be all right. An outright lie;
I have no idea what will happen after this. She reaches a hand up to clasp
one of mine, then buries her head in my shoulder. For this moment, this
man is giving me a perversion of my deepest desires. It would be unfair to
ask me to refrain.

I turn her gently onto her back, promising myself that I will be ever
so gentle with her, that she will find joy. Chantal has gone still. Her eyes
are closed, and she looks terrifyingly defenseless. I bend to drop butterfly
kisses on her cheek, her neck, her shoulder. Carefully I avoid her lips,
though I ache to kiss. Somehow I think that would be too much. For her,
and for me. Her nipples are soft pools of darkness in the golden expanse of

her torso. I lick my way down to them, nipping gently until they stand erect against my tongue. She has begun to move a little, confused by her body's reactions. But she voices no protest. My frail love has no way of understanding this night, her only hope to trust in me to keep her safe.

His breathing is loud in the room, and as I kiss lower and lower on her sweet body, the first moan comes from him. It is a sound of pure frustration, and I am surprised that he restrains himself. Then I am lost in the scent of her rising up beneath me, the brush of my breasts along her long legs, the caress of my curling hair against my cheek. And the greatest joy is that she is responding to my touch, my tongue, my kiss. She is arching underneath me, tangling long fingers in my hair, running nails across the tender places of my neck. The lamp flickers wildly in the room; as she comes moaning in my mouth we arch together suddenly still.

Chantal relaxes beneath me, her still-heavy breaths sounding. I cannot hear him, I realize. I half-raise, and twist my body up into the wind from the fan. There is enough light to see clearly that he is not there. The knife lies, discarded, well within arm's reach. He has closed the door behind him. And suddenly I am battling the impulse to reach out and take the knife and hold it to her sweet flesh, gaining a night of unbearable pleasure as she fulfills my every desire.

And also gaining her hatred. I shake my head, dismissing the last foolish thoughts. This will have to be enough. Her trust, her faith. Her slick body molded to my own. The memory of her arching against me. And the chance that this night has changed her mind about what she wants....

I lie down against her, realizing that she is somehow, impossibly, asleep. I am suddenly eager to join her.

***

The phone rings. I get up to answer, knowing who it will be.

"Forgive me," he says. "I should have stayed with your plan. Bringing the knife was a mistake. You were both too beautiful, and I got... carried away." He pauses, embarrassed. "I'll buy you a new shirt."

"Forgiven." I say, and hang up.

How can I condemn him? I asked him to come, after all. I go back to the bed and gather her into my arms. She murmurs in her sleep and cuddles closer. I hold her tight in a protective embrace, so that nobody will ever hurt her.

TORN SHAPES OF DESIRE

The shape of her love
is gut-wrenching.

Unspoken fear that
this time
will be the last
he will go back
to his wife
leaving her alone
in emptiness.

She dances on knives
abandoning everything
for touch of warm hands
fevered lips
whispered promises.

Though she knows
better than anyone
that he is a liar.

Willingly
she dances
till feet lie torn
conscience is screaming
and guilt is the shape
of her love.

FLEEING GODS

Helena struggled out of sleep, blinking her eyes hazily against the darkened room. It had been a most vivid dream. Since she'd left her spineless husband and the regular supply of dull sex, she'd often had erotic dreams. Somehow none had been quite this... explicit. A tongue had licked her instep, her toes. Teeth had nibbled on her calves. She had almost been able to feel the muscled body, the sensuous hands caressing her thighs, her hips. She could almost hear his heavy panting, and smell his strong breath.

Actually, she could still smell that strong breath, that unmistakable mixture of strong spirits and poor oral hygiene. There was a strong scent of aroused male in the room. Helena suddenly sat up and switched on her halogen lamp, ready to grab it and crack it on the skull of any would-be rapist.

As the light flooded the room, an immense man reared up on the bed and away from her, raising a hairy arm to block his eyes from the light.

"Shut that off, wench! You'll ruin the mood!"

Wench? What kind of man calls a woman wench? Helena relaxed a little, still retaining her firm grip on the lamp, and peered at the impressive stranger in her bedroom.

"What are you doing here?" she asked him, quite calmly, she thought.

"Seducing you!" he thundered. "What does it look like I'm doing?" He lowered his arm a bit, piercing blue eyes blinking in the light like those of a dazed deer. Helena stared intently at him, hungrily drinking in the obvious strength in those arms, that chest. The man was positively bristling with hair, and muscles bulged under the thick brown coat. Something else bulged too, an enormous penis that stood out proudly from his naked body. Helena had been married for seven years, and bar-hopping for three, but she had never seen anything to match this before. She licked her lips.

He blinked at her, looking a little confused. Then he seemed to gather himself together. He started shouting again.

"Fear not, fair maiden. I am the greatest of lovers, renowned in seven kingdoms and across seventy seas. No harm will come to thee!"

Helena winced at the volume. "Could you lower your voice a little?" she asked, as she started to shift her body, preparatory to sitting up. The man immediately flung himself down on her, pinning her to the bed. Helena just lay there, enjoying the weight of his body on hers, the teasing scritch of curly chest hair against her nipples.

"My apologies, maiden, but I cannot have you turning into a bull, or a swan, or trying to run away" he said, in a voice slightly softer than before.

A bull? A swan? A strange suspicion started dancing through Helena's head. "Just what did you say your name was?" she asked him.

The man's chest swelled proudly, incidentally crushing her breasts beneath it. "I am Zeus, ruler of Olympus, seducer of maidens, wieldier of the thunderbolt... and you shall not escape me!"

"Why would I want to?" Helena practically cooed, as she laced her arms around his thick neck. That would explain how he got into her locked bedroom, the odd dream she'd been having... it would explain a lot of things. She began rubbing her naked body against his, maneuvering so he could slide that gorgeous tool into the place where it belonged.

"Sorry?" he said. His voice suddenly seemed much less like massive thundering, and more like a pitiful squeak. He held his body very stiff as he stared down at her. While stiff was good in some ways, his stillness was somewhat of a problem now, as she couldn't get to quite the position she needed. "Are you not afraid of me? Will you not shift your form into a thousand others so as to escape? Will you not turn into a tree, a pebble, a breath of breeze?"

"Honey, I can't shift my form into even one other." Helena replied. She raked her nails along his back, and writhed her body underneath his, hoping to stimulate a response. His response wasn't quite what she expected.

"But it is simple. Even the shepherd maids of Greece knew how. Let me show you," he said. And with that, she felt an odd sort of twist in her brain, strange enough to make her pause a second in her feverish groping. Suddenly she knew how to change forms, how to become a thousand creatures of wind and flesh and earth. Zeus smiled in triumph above her. "Now, will you run?" he asked.

"Mmm... I don't think so," Helena said. With that, she used her newfound knowledge to stretch her body, adding several inches to her height, and not so incidentally enabling her to finally slip that stiff penis inside her dripping cunt. Helena gasped then, and bit down on his rock-hard shoulder. She started to slide back and forth, almost gnawing on his skin as she did so.

"But they always run," Zeus said. He sounded dismayed. "I cannot believe human women have changed so in the mere millennia that Hera and I spent travelling ... surely you are unnatural, a freak?"

Helena kept moving as she replied, "Well, my appetite's maybe a bit bigger than most women's, but I think I'm pretty typical nowadays." Suddenly, that feeling of delicious fullness started to disappear. Helena looked up in sudden suspicion. "Hey, if you're a god, surely you can keep it up?"

Zeus started to pull himself away. "You are a hellish imitation of a true woman. I will go and find a more feminine being in whom to spend my heavenly seed. You cannot expect me to perform with a creature as un-womanly as yourself. It would be... unnatural!"

Helena suddenly clung even harder, wrapping her long (extremely long) legs around his muscular form. "Not so fast, boy. You look to be the best lay I've had in a long time." Helena's mind continued the sentence; 'with potentially infinite endurance.' "You're not getting away until I get what you promised earlier. And not until I get it several times!"

Zeus moaned in dismay, and suddenly changed himself into a porcu-pine. But Helena changed her skin into bristly fur, and stuck to him like Velcro. He wailed in horror, and changed himself into a lightning bolt. But she changed into a storm, and blew out all the windows as she surrounded him. Zeus moaned as he turned into a waterfall, pouring out of her forty-seventh floor windows. But she turned into a river right below him, and engulfed his sweet essence. It was then that he really started to run.

Helena chased him down the highway, causing the early morning traffic jams to become early morning wrecking sites, as the heavenly dawn filled the sky. Irate businessmen in suits leaning out their car windows could hear a male voice, whimpering on the wind as the pair disappeared over the horizon. It was clearly calling, "Hera? Saaaaaaaave meeeeeeeee........" The ones who listened carefully even heard a soft chuckle of what might have been goddess laughter as they hurriedly pulled their heads back inside, and quickly rolled up the windows.

COBALT BLUE

By late September, I will be gone, and that
love that wraps us now in warm arms may wither
under the weight of time. I know that as well as you,
even though I hide behind closed eyes.

Gather me close, my dear. For a little while
let me pretend belief in forever, in happily ever
after. After all, such are the fairy tales of love's
sweet sorcery on which we are raised. That hearts can
stop time together, that distance is powerless.

Grassy fields and summer sun lie still before us.
One still November night we met, and though I admit it
bitter that less than a single year is to be ours,
let us not waste the seasons we have in
early sorrow. If my next November is to be as blue as
the glasses you once gave me, the memory of
summer will light my rooms, and I will raise a glass to you.

(for David)

COLOPHON

This book was created electronically using Adobe Frame-Maker under Windows 95 (on a system with 133 mhz Pentium and 64 mb RAM, in case you really care). Interior text set in Adobe Caslon, with camera ready copy produced on a LaserJet 4MP. Interior photographs were supplied as prints and half-toned by the printer. Printed on recycled paper. Cover created in Adobe Illustrator, Adobe Photoshop and QuarkXPress on Macintosh.

"I chose the Caslon font because it had the slightly 'romantic' look I wanted. Only after that choice did I discover the history of the font, and how it has been favored by some of the greatest freedom lovers of history. The first printings of both the Declaration of Independence and the Constitution were set in Caslon, and Ben Franklin used Caslon almost exclusively. I visited Independence Hall and the Liberty Bell during production of the book. There was something special about that visit, somehow different from other times I'd been there. I felt myself to be in very good company, publishing this book in the modern Philadelphia suburbs." -d.l.

About the Author

Mary Anne Mohanraj is currently attending a Creative Writing MFA program at Mills College near San Francisco. Born in Sri Lanka in 1971 and raised in Connecticut, she received a B.A. in English from the University of Chicago in 1993, and has been writing and publishing ever since. Her work appears in a variety of forums—from staid poetry journals to science fiction anthologies to hard-core porn magazines. A complete list is available on her Web page, under Publications. Recently she has had "Goddess Blessing" in Masquerade's *Floating Worlds* anthology, and "Fleeing Gods" will appear in Circlet Press's forthcoming *Sex Magick II* anthology. She is currently working on a fantasy novel, tentatively titled *Dreams By Lamplight*.

About the Photographer

Tracy Lee has focused her artistic energies on photography since she first took up a camera in high school. Ten years later and she's still going strong. While her full time job as a graphic artist keeps her busy during the day it is behind—and in front of—a lens where Tracy prefers to spend her hours. She lives outside of Washington, D.C. with her husband, daughter, and their two dogs.